# Eros Unzipped

## Dirk Mourningwood

Thanks, Linda.
You should have listened, but look where we're at now.

# Introduction

Many of these stories are loosely based on actual events. Emphasis on "loosely". Prepare yourself for a few toxic or not-exactly-consensual relations. The goal was to tap into fantasy, and fantasy isn't always tidy.

Always practice safe sex.

**Trigger warnings** feel almost unnecessary to include in a book of eight male-on-male erotica stories. Prepare yourself for graphic sexual acts and strong language. The sex isn't always safe; those involved aren't always sober. There are age gaps and power dynamics, but no one is forced in the end.

# Contents

# Swish Pants

I COULD ALWAYS HEAR him coming. I could hear the swish, swish, swish of his polyester track pants from down the hall. This was my first semester of college, and I don't remember how I got in the habit of just leaving my dorm room's door to the hall open if I was in the living room. It was convenient for friends to stop by and just walk in, but also let me know when my roommate was walking from the elevator.

Not that I cared when he came and went. Well, I cared when he suddenly disappeared, but I'm not at that part of the story yet. We'd barely spoken since the hectic move-in day. I only knew his last name from the lease paperwork and never knew his major. Probably business. We shared a two-bedroom apartment with a bunkbed in each room. I never was totally sure of the names of the other two guys I lived with.

But swish pants was Raj, and he had the lower bunk. I would have joked about it, being a top later in life, but this was long before I came out. Long before I cashed in my V-card, but not before I knew what I thought I wanted. Raj and I said our pleasantries in passing but otherwise didn't say anything to each other.

After two weeks of sleeping in the top bunk, my first time away from home, I woke Friday morning to the whole bed rhythmically shaking. At least it felt that way. I noticed every motion Raj made below me but never complained or told him about it. I felt him get in and out, roll over, and now I felt every stroke as he was, I was very sure, jerking off three feet below me.

I completely locked up, straining my hearing to confirm what I assumed was happening. Moving carefully, I caught the time, 7:09 am. It took everything not to laugh or offer to give him a hand. It felt like twenty minutes that he was cranking at it down there. I heard all the tell-tale sounds of wanking dry, of squeezing a crown dripping with precum, and quickened breath. The shaking became erratic, and he exhaled in quick bursts. He moved more gently, then swung his legs off the bed, swishing out the door and to the bathroom across the hall.

7:14 am.

Okay, so not twenty minutes, but it felt like it.

My cock was as hard as ever, and maybe a bit confused by the interaction. I'd idly touched mine as Raj wrecked his but didn't do more out of pure shock.

I heard the shower running. My alarm would be going off in a minute anyway, so I made sure I was tucked back in my briefs before tossing back the sheets and dropping my legs over the edge of the bunk. Pulling on sweats and grabbing my gym bag, I was out the door while Raj was still in the shower.

"The fuck, Marshal! He was jerking off right under you? That's so fucked!"

I couldn't stop myself from telling the story to Samantha, my best friend from high school and the only person I knew coming into college. Well, I told her what Raj did, but not how I thought it was one of the hottest moments of my life until then. I hushed her from where we slowly walked on the treadmills, but the rec center was mostly empty at this time of day.

"Raj is pretty hot, though," she continued. "That beard, and he always wears tight shirts, if you noticed."

Oh, I noticed.

"If he does it again, you should peek. Tell me what he's got going on down there." She winked.

I laughed. "You slut." I don't know how she didn't know I was gay. It turns out she did know but was waiting for me to tell her. Samantha's a total sweetie. But the thought of peeking turned a wheel in my brain. "Do you think he'll do it again?"

"We're not even a month into the semester. If he's so shameless to fucking wank off staring at the bottom of your mattress, he'll do it again."

"I wonder why he didn't do it in the bathroom. He knows I get up at 7:30."

"Because he wants you to know he's doing it, that's why. He's an exhibitionist." She tapped my chest. "Next time, get out of bed, go for a drink of water, act like nothing's up. See what he does."

Next time. There was a better chance than not that there would be a next time. Maybe this wasn't even the first time. How many times had he done it without waking me? Maybe it's a daily ritual, but today was more vigorous.

"What do you think about that?" Samantha asked, and I realized I was just staring into space, thinking about Raj. I was also starting to chub and couldn't do that in sweatpants.

"I'll do my best to get you a full report," I chuckled. Even as I said it, I doubted I would tell her if I saw anything. On the first day in the apartment, I had the longest conversation I'd had with Raj to date. All while he was only wearing white briefs. I'd held a pillow in my lap, sitting in my bunk, all while trying not to stare at his small nipples, trim waist, or the hair on his inner thigh. More evidence that he likes to be looked at, perhaps. I told Samantha a lot, but some things remained between roommates. Perhaps I shouldn't have told her about that morning. I excused myself from our morning treadmill stroll and fled to the locker room, beating off quickly in a bathroom stall when my boner refused to go down.

That evening, the other roommates, who didn't speak much English, were having a party in the living room, so I sat in my bunk, the room lit only by my dim laptop screen. Mom said doing that would ruin my eyes, but why live on campus if not to defy your parents?

I heard the swish, swish, swish, and Raj entered, finishing up his phone conversation in what I assumed was his native tongue. He snapped the phone closed and tossed it to his bed.

He flicked on the light, startling when he saw me. "Hey, Marsh."

"Hey, Raj."

Deep talks.

"Are you going home this weekend?" he asked, as I'd driven the hour home the last few weekends for laundry.

"No, I need to focus on this CAD project." I waved a finger at my laptop.

"Cool. It might be a quiet one. I have some reading to catch up on." His eyes were locked onto mine. Without breaking eye contact, he pulled off his shirt, tossing it in his bin. "I'm hoping to sleep in." He held my gaze just a breath longer, then turned for the bathroom, closing the door behind him.

Weird.

By then, it was almost midnight. He'd be doing his nightly twenty-minute routine of beard oils and skin care. I took the time to shut down my laptop and settle into bed with a book.

He swished into the room on time, closing the door behind him. "I'm going to the laundry mat tomorrow," he said, pulling my attention. Not that I wasn't already peeking at him, but now I didn't have to hide it. "You can come with me if you want." Holding my eye again, he slipped his thumbs into his track pants waistband, sliding them down and stepping out of them. When he straightened, he grabbed a fistful of his briefs, tugging down, adjusting as any guy might ten times a day without noticing. He switched off the overhead light and he was shaking the bed, getting in below me before I fully processed it.

"I go at four or five. Let me know. Good night, Marsh."

"Night, Raj."

I strained my hearing, wondering if any of his little movements that rocked my upper bunk might be the first movements to his masturbation, but eventually, sleep won.

The clock was already in my field of vision when I opened my eyes—7:48 am. My bed swayed with Raj's movements.

Samantha's suggestion popped up as fast as my erection. Get out of bed, act natural, and see what happens.

I sat up. He didn't stop.

I yawned loudly. He kept going.

I dropped my legs over the edge, and my bed's wobble stopped. Hopping down, I left for the kitchen, leaving the bedroom door open. The living room was still a mess from the other roommates' party. Plastic cups and plates covered every surface. Two strangers were passed out on the couch, but whatever. They'd clean it up. I poured a glass of water, taking a long drink just as I stepped back through my bedroom doorway. Raj was lying on his side facing me, eyes closed, but didn't stir as I stepped a foot on the edge of his mattress, by his legs, to climb up as I always did.

A moment later, I felt him roll over, starting again.

He knows I'm awake. He doesn't know I can feel everything, but I could still hear him. If anything, he was louder than the day before, breathing hard.

Fuck it. He was jerking off, and I knew he was jerking off. I'd do it too.

Lifting my hips, I pulled my sheets, sweats, and briefs to my knees, tucking my t-shirt up to my ribs. One hand wrapped my shaft as the other cupped my balls, brushing my thumb down the center of my sack. I didn't try to be quiet but I also didn't try to make too much noise. I added my rhythm to his, and it didn't take me long. My quickened gasps sounded thunderous when I came across my belly, echoed by his seconds later.

The image came to me, beautiful and surreal, of us three feet apart, ropes of cum shot across our abdomens. Totally apart, yet together in our shared activity.

He jumped up and fled to the bathroom. I strained for a sock from the top of my laundry bin, cleaning up as best I could and tucking the sheets to my throat just as he returned. I could barely see him in the early light, and he surely couldn't see my face with the window behind me, but he still locked his eyes on mine with a smirk. He looked away for just a breath, tapping a finger on his teeth. Then he was looking at me again. Thumbs in his briefs, he ripped them to the floor, grabbed his flaccid cock and sack in one fistful, gave it a quick tug, and slipped back into bed. I'd never seen an uncircumcised dick before, and it was lovely.

I wanted to stay in bed forever, waiting for him to get up first, but my alarm beeped at 8:30. I slapped that quiet faster than I ever had before. Why did I even have an alarm set for Saturday? I still didn't want to get up before him. I had to know if he'd just get up, stretching, cock and balls on display for me. Grabbing my laptop, I shuffled to sit up and remember where I'd left off on my project the night before, but my brain was a haze from the mix of sleep and hormones. When Raj finally got up, he sat on the edge of his bed, invisible to me unless I leaned over mine. I heard him pulling on swishy pants before gathering other clothes and leaving for the bathroom. All without a word to me. He went from there to the kitchen and out.

My first Saturday in the dorm apartment rushed by. I got breakfast, showered, and plodded along with homework until a couple of friends stopped by for lunch. By the time I got back, the living room was cleaned up from the party the night before. Before I knew it, Raj was back and asked if I wanted to go to the laundry mat. My first reaction was to decline, but now I had cum soaking across the top layers in my bin. I didn't want to take that home to put in mom's washer.

I brought my laptop, and we said nothing in the twenty-minute walk across campus, bags of dirty clothes slapping against our backs with every step. Groups of students played frisbee or hackysack, sat in study groups, or made out in pairs. The laundry mat was empty when we stepped onto the linoleum floors lit by buzzing fluorescents. As we dumped our first armfuls into the washer, stained with our shared loads that morning, my mind screamed for answers, or at least for me to ask the question. Why did you show me your dick? Can you show it to me again? Can I touch it?

"It's always empty here at this time," Raj said quietly, almost to himself. "Everyone's at the game or filling up the bars."

"Do you come every week?"

He nodded. Dropping his washer's lid, he pumped in a few quarters and turned to me, locking his gaze like he had that morning.

"I want to show you something, Marsh."

"Okay." I fed quarters into the machine and twisted the nob to start it rumbling.

He jerked his head toward a door labeled "Employees."

It was just a storage closet, but the floor was tidy enough to move around a little. He flicked on a harsh overhead bulb and closed the door behind us.

"Did you see anything this morning?" he asked casually.

I swallowed hard. "I did."

He leaned back against a rack of cleaning supplies with his elbows spread along the shelf. "What did you see?"

"I saw... well, it was dark." I stepped back, leaning against the shelves on the other side of the room, arms crossed.

"It's bright in here. Do you want a better look?"

My eyes flicked to the naked bulb overhead while my palms were getting sweaty and my dick hard. I swallowed the lump in my throat. "Just look?"

"I like being seen, being looked at," he chuckled. "What else would you do, Marsh?" He lifted the bottom of his t-shirt, showing me his thin waist, pulling the tight cotton slowly up and over his head.

I stared at those small nipples. "I don't know," I muttered.

His thumbs were in his track pants, pushing them down. "You don't know?" His cock bulged against his tight briefs, and his thumbs were in his waistband. Suddenly, his uncut dick was pointing straight up at me, pink head shining with precum around the fold of foreskin. Sprouting from a forest of dark, straight pubes, I wanted to grab it, feel how it would be to stroke an uncut cock. "How about you show me you?"

My thumbs were under the elastic of my waistband. After another frantic breath of tugging my hoodie over my ears, we were naked and hard in the cramped storeroom, close enough that our dicks nearly touched.

I expected some comment, always self-conscious about how I bent to the right, but Raj was silent. He lowered one hand to stroke under the length of his cock, gently teasing it. I wanted little more in that moment than to stroke him, weigh his balls in my palm. Once my eyes finally found his again, I saw he was already waiting for me. He flashed his gaze, then he started stroking, slow and full, eyes never breaking from mine, barely blinking. I mirrored him, not fully understanding the appeal but certainly not begrudging it. His other hand fumbled for a paper towel roll, tearing off a wad for us each.

Raj's dark eyes bore into mine, wordlessly demanding that I not shift my gaze from his as I watched the sweat bead across his dark brow down to the cord of muscle popping from his neck, but no lower. His breath quickened as he came, and that pushed me over the edge. We came seconds apart. Never breaking eye contact.

He took the paper towel from me, not caring how my cum smeared through his fingers and shoved them deep into the waste basket in a corner. Still without a word, we dressed and went back to our laundry. I worked on my CAD project while he read a history book. We went our own ways for dinner and never mentioned it when I turned out the light and climbed up to my bunk.

For the next three months, several times a week, one of us would wake the other by jerking off in our bunk. The other would join. We usually managed to finish at the same rate. I stopped going home on weekends to step into that supply closet with him instead. On the third week, I told him, "I want to feel your cock." He let me, and I worked us in rhythm. Two more weeks, I stacked our cocks in my hand and jerked us off together, all while never breaking eye contact.

I said I wanted to kiss him. He didn't say no, but he wouldn't kiss me back, so I stopped before long.

We both started sleeping naked, making a point to strip and dress with the other watching, but we never touched each other in the dorm. He actually never touched me at all. In our last time in the storage room, with the snow piling up against the wall of windows out front, I wanted so badly to suck his cock, to pull back that foreskin and taste his dick, but he wanted to keep eye contact the whole time, said it only worked for him with eye contact.

I returned on January 3 to find Raj's bed stripped and his side of the closet empty. I had a moment of anger, something like betrayal, that he would just disappear. That shifted to denial, but even his beard oils and toothbrush were gone. Sadness settled for a while, thinking about what we had and didn't have and what was now gone from my life. A half-hour later, as I was walking down the ten flights to the housing office on the main floor. They confirmed Raj Singh moved out over break but couldn't tell me if he'd graduated, transferred, or dropped out, only that he hadn't moved to another apartment. That last bit was a relief, that he hadn't moved to escape me. The manager said it was unlikely someone else would move in mid-year, so I had the room to myself. She even offered to have the extra bed removed. I told her that wasn't necessary.

"Fuck you, Marsh! You got the room to yourself?" Samantha punched my arm from the treadmill next to mine. "They added a girl to my room over break. Bitch has to sleep on a cot."

She gossiped about the new roommate, who smelled like cabbage, and I let my mind drift, wondering as I had for a week about what happened to Raj and if I should be concerned.

"You never told me if you caught him jerking again," said Samantha. "That first time couldn't have been the one and only."

After holding it from her for months, I couldn't tell her the truth now. So, I did what any closeted gay man gets great at. I deflected. "I guess now that he's gone, I can tell you. I did see him naked a few times."

Samantha jumped to the runners along her treadmill and grabbed my arm like a vice grip.

"Tell me everything. Did you just catch him coming out of the shower, or did he show off like the exhibitionist we know he is?"

I slowed my machine, laughing. There was no one near us, but I still whispered, again not answering her question. "He has little nipples and isn't circumcised."

Samantha blew a raspberry. "I could have guessed just." She begged me for more. Length, girth, amount and shape of pubes, ball hanginess. I refused to give her more details, citing a made-up roommate confidentiality agreement. Samantha offered to tell me anything I wanted about the new cabbage girl, but she knew that was a deal I didn't care about.

It turned out to be a blessing in disguise. While in it, I would have never admitted how oddly toxic our situation was. I never heard from Raj again, but I started the winter semester focused on my classmates I'd ignored while lusting after my roommate, making friends and connections that I should college. It wasn't long before I met Jorge, and I wasn't alone in that room for long. But that's another story for another time.

# Hitchhiker

BEAT FROM A WEEK of class and a major group project, I just wanted to get home, play with my dog, start the first load of laundry, and sprawl out on my childhood bed. Dad would probably make me a late dinner. He usually overdid it, vying for my affection, and I didn't stop him.

The drive home should have taken just over two hours, but I was going on four after waiting on an accident and then construction. I wasn't about to pull over and drag out my spiral-bound maps to find a different route. Now, it was just starting to rain. I'd only been driving a few years and didn't want to deal with this. It was so late. At least I was basically alone on the highway now.

My exit was next, thank god.

Slowing on the offramp, I passed a Honda Civic that, even in the dark, I saw was missing a tire. Ahead, my headlight swept across a guy in jeans and a chunky wool sweater. He looked like he might have been on his way to a work holiday party before his car broke down. Now, he walked backward, holding out a thumb.

Hitchhiking? I didn't know anyone actually did that anymore. Even at a distance, I saw the pleading in his eyes. I was probably the first car to pass in a half hour, and the rain was picking up.

He could go back to his car to get out of the rain, wait until morning, and walk to the gas station a mile off the exit.

Or I could drive him now.

My foot decided for me, slamming on the brake. I reversed to catch him halfway and reached over to unlock the passenger door.

He yanked the door open and dropped in the seat, brushing back his wet mop of curly, dirty-blond hair.

His cologne hit me, a mix of sandalwood and other fragrances I couldn't name. It wasn't the cheap sprays the guys in my chemistry lab doused themselves in. This was richer, applied precisely.

The overhead light was starting to dim, highlighting the green in his eyes.

"I can't thank you enough," he said. "I thought I'd be out there all night."

"Not a problem. I live around here. Can I drive you to the gas station or something?"

"That would be great. My phone died." He showed me his Motorolla and tucked it back in the front pocket of his jeans.

I put the car back in drive. "Were you heading somewhere? Not much out this way except cows and corn."

"Party at a friend's house, but it's probably over by now." He wrung his hands together as if trying to get warm. "I should have brought a coat."

I flicked the heat to high. "Is it close? I could drop you there."

"I couldn't ask you to do that."

The light was green at the end of the ramp, but I stopped, waiting to know which way to turn. "You're not, I'm offering. Better to stay with friends than a gas station attendant. If the house is dark, I'll bring you back." I nodded to the GasWay Plus lit in the distance.

"Thanks, sure. Take a right. I'm Bennet, by the way."

"Arthur."

"Thanks, Arthur."

I noticed the shiver in his voice.

"Are you still cold?" The heat wouldn't go any higher, and I was sweating.

"Yeah, my sweater's soaked." He picked at the chunky wool.

"Take it off, warm up for a few minutes."

I stopped at a red light, the last for miles out this way. Bennet unbuckled his seatbelt and gathered the thick wool at his waist, leaning forward to pull it over his head. I glanced over and watched the dim light from the dash gauges and the red light play across his back muscles. The fabric waded up awkwardly across his shoulders, and I reached to help him tug it off.

"Thanks." He sat back and buckled just as the light turned green. He grinned at me, and I had to tear my eyes from the fine hair across his chest to focus back on the road. "The turn's up here somewhere." He leaned forward, squinting in the faint light and holding his hands over the heat vents.

"It's just farms out this way."

Another mile passed before Bennet asked me to slow down. "I think it's up here."

We crawled by a farmhouse a quarter mile from the road with a single light in an upstairs room.

He shook his head. "I'm sorry, Arthur. We might have missed it." His eye lingered on the farmhouse as we passed.

"You don't know where your friend lives?"

Bennet leaned back with a huff. "I guess not. I was supposed to be here hours ago. Could you take me back to the gas station?"

I could. I definitely could. I'd have to pass the gas station on the way home. I'd drop him off, leave him standing in the cold rain holding a soaked, wadded up, chunky wool sweater, and never think about him again.

Except that I would.

No, I shouldn't. Besides enjoying the vibe I got from Bennet, I honestly wanted to help. But inviting total strangers to stay the night is the first scene of enough horror movies. Even strangers with hair I'd love to tangle my fingers in.

I stopped and made a U-turn in the middle of the deserted road. Within a few minutes, I was pulling into the GasWay Plus lot, and Bennet was fumbling to find his sweater's neck hole.

"Sorry you couldn't find your friend's place." He looked good in the fluorescents of the gas station, casting harsh shadows over his pecs.

Bennet smiled over at me, still struggling with his sweater. "Thanks, Arthur. Can I buy you a candy bar or something? Chip in for some gas?"

A rusted-out pick-up truck rumbled into the space next to the passenger door. The three snap-back and camo-wearing rednecks glared as they walked in front of my car, hitching up their pants that probably smelled like deer piss, not at all shy about the pistols holstered on their hips. "Fucking queers," one yelled, getting a laugh from his buddies.

Fuck no.

I popped the car into reverse. "I'm taking you to my place. You can borrow something dry, charge your phone, and sleep in my brother's bed."

Bennet looked at me, shocked and maybe a little nervous. "That... Really, Arthur? I mean, thanks. You live with your brother?" His gaze lingered on the rough men as we returned to the road.

"No, it's my dad's house. Sam and I shared a room, but he moved out a few years ago. But the room has private access, so you won't have to deal with my dad. He can be... a lot. He means well."

My babbling might have calmed him from thinking I was a serial killer who preyed on hitchhikers. He relaxed, leaning against the door to face me. "Yeah, thank you. I'll call a tow and be out at first light."

I couldn't stop my eyes moving over him when I pulled up to that same red light. He took a deep breath, stretching an arm behind his head and flexing his bicep. "I'm warmer already." He returned the same energy that I sent at him. Did he want me as much as I wanted him? It was a dangerous question to ask when getting it wrong might get you a fist in the face or worse.

The rednecks with pistols came to mind.

The rain was a steady, windless downpour when we pulled into the driveway a few minutes later. Dad's truck was missing. I didn't specifically tell him I'd be coming, so he was probably out with his new girlfriend, along with my dog. Deciding I'd get my bags and laundry in the morning, we rushed up the side stairs for me to fumble with the keys. We spilled into my room, laughing to brush off how long it took to open the door with Bennet hovering near me.

Flicking on the light, I held back signs of embarrassment. The bright wall paint, the hammock of stuffed animals, the Star Trek sheets on my bed, Star Wars on Sam's. How did we never update through high school?

"You're soaked now, too," Bennet laughed, tugging at my shirt. He passed me to cup his hands over his eyes, looking out the window toward the back of the house. "I don't see any other houses."

"We're on about thirty acres. The nearest house is a half mile away." I pulled off my coat and leaned back against the corner post of my bed's footboard.

Bennet turned, laying his sweater along the edge of my empty clothes hamper. "Do you ever want to stand in the rain?" He ran his thumbs under his jeans' waistband, adjusting them to sit slightly lower, showing the V trail along his hips. He was trim but not too muscled. Maybe a wrestler or swimmer. Short hair disappeared into his dark jeans low around his thin waist.

I chuckled. "Stand in the rain? I seem to remember that you're half naked because you got wet and cold."

"Only half." He crossed his right arm across his chest, holding his left shoulder, flexing his arm again. Clearly intentional.

Standing in the rain at one in the morning. What a stupid idea.

He bit his lower lip.

Fuck it.

I pulled off my t-shirt, stepping to drop it beside his sweater, and came close enough to slip a hand around Bennet's side. "Let's go for a walk." I jerked my chin toward the door.

He stopped me with one palm flat on my stomach, and the other hand worked his belt buckle.

Sensible. Denin takes forever to dry. I stepped out of my boots, pulled off my socks, and dropped my pants as he did. Just a couple of young guys standing an arm span apart, drinking in the sight of each other's bodies. The movement in his boxers answered my earlier question.

He dove out the door, and I ran after him. The shock of cold stole my breath for a heartbeat, but then I couldn't feel anything. We stumbled down the steps, laughing at nothing. I took his hand, splashing through mud that sucked at our ankles, and led him to the back of the house.

"It's beautiful," he said. We stood overlooking the little valley bathed in moonlight. Growing up here, I never thought much of it, but it felt a little different now, with the low hills lit by infrequent, silent lightning.

"We should have put your phone on the—"

His lips were on mine, hands across my back, crushing us together.

The shock only lasted a breath before I had one hand in his hair, the other sliding down his back, under his boxer's waistband, to take a handful of his firm ass. The discomfort of being cold or wet blasted from my mind, with his tongue sliding across mine.

His lips trailed across my cheek, to my ear, teeth clamping lightly on my lobe. "Do you ever want to be blown by a stranger in the rain?"

"You're not a complete stranger, Bennet," I breathed into his ear.

"Are you sure that's my name?"

Creepy, but point taken. No, I hadn't been blown by a stranger in the rain, but...

My hand ran through his hair, pushing down, and he eagerly dropped. He did it slowly, letting his hands and lips trace across my chest, my ribs, and my belly. His fingers pinched the leg of my trunks and tugged them down slowly.

Bennet wasted no time, taking my swollen cock in one hand, lifting it to run his tongue along my balls and slowly up my shaft.

I tilted my head back, closing my eyes from the steady rain and the pleasure Bennet was inflicting upon my cock. He worked it in a slow rhythm, gripping his fingers in time with the motion. His mouth focused on my sack, licking his tongue from the back, sucking one ball at a time between his lips.

My hands slid through his hair, feeling the wet curls between my fingers, tightening into fists.

His warm tongue, in contrast to the chill rain, slid up my cock and down to take me into his throat. In and out slowly so I could feel his throat close in around my head.

He jerked back with a choking cough. I should feel bad when that happens, but it only made me smirk.

I looked down at Bennet, coughing and wiping rain from his eyes.

"Sorry," he said as he stood, still wiping his eyes. "That didn't work how I thought it would. You weren't close, were you?"

I wasn't, but I wasn't about to say that out loud. I stepped out of my shorts and bent to pick them up. Naked, I slipped my fingers through his, guiding us toward the house.

He pulled us to a stop before we made it three steps and dropped his underwear, kicking it up to catch it with a smirk. Lit by the moon behind the clouds and flashes of lightning, I took in the sight of him. I wanted to lick the water off every square inch of him, but where to start?

"How about a walk naked in the rain?" He spread his arms and walked backward from me.

Directly toward the edge of the hill.

I called out, rushing forward a step, but his foot slipped, and he fell backward. I was at him a few breaths later, twenty feet down the hill, both covered in mud. He was laughing, rubbing muddy hands over his face. I couldn't help but join him once I realized he wasn't hurt.

"I'm no good at being sexy," Bennet laughed.

I knelt between his legs, pushing them apart, sliding my cock against his. My fingers clasped his again, holding them over his head in the mud. "You're doing a fine enough job from where I'm standing. Kneeling."

He crossed his ankles behind my hips, pulling me closer. Rain pelted my back, running rivers down my arms. Still holding him, I kissed his nipples and nipped at the softer skin at his ribs, making him squirm.

This was insane. I thought I'd start a load of laundry, jerk off, and be in bed a half hour ago. Not grinding my dick against a hot stranger's in the mud behind my house. If this were payment for picking up a hitchhiker, I'd do it all the time.

"I want you to cum on me," he moaned. "Can you do that?"

I wanted to cum in him. Or me on him while he was in me. I'd take him any which way.

Releasing his hands, I took both our cocks in a single grip, working us like I liked it. Tilting my head back to let the rain pour across my face and down my chest, my other hand slipped between his legs, cupping his balls. Fuck they were huge. His hands left clumsy, muddy streaks across my chest and down my stomach. A lot of what he did felt clumsy.

He gasped. "Shit!"

His balls tightened in my hand, and his cock spasmed in my other as his back arched and legs squeezed around my hips. When he started to relax, I dropped his cock to finish myself off with a dozen strokes, shooting blind in the dark.

I leaned down to kiss him again, then sat back on my heels, waiting for a flash of lightning to see the lines of cum mixed with mud across his belly and chest, almost to his throat.

I tried to slow my breathing and could feel the rain's chill setting in. We'd have to find our underwear, fumble back to the house, clean up, and go to bed between the Star Trek and Wars sheets. Not knowing what words would move us forward, I took his hands and stood, pulling him with me.

"That was so good," he finally said.

I pulled him close to kiss him at the bottom of the stairs. "I've never thought to take a walk in the rain, much less have sex in it."

Bennet chuckled awkwardly in response.

I tossed him a towel and ran our clothes to the washing machine on the main level, still naked. When I returned with a box of crackers, he stood in front of the mirror in my bathroom, the towel around his feet. Muddy water still ran from his curls, but I could clean up the floor tomorrow. For now, he was nice to look at.

"I didn't know what to expect, but thank you, Arthur."

I moved beside him, leaning against the counter. "What to expect about what? Sex in the rain?" I smirked.

"My... I haven't done that before." He turned fully toward me, eyes lingering on my limp dick.

"Neither have I, I... Oh..."

"I'm a virgin."

"Was." That explained his clumsiness. Did I seriously take a guy's V-card without knowing? Dammit, I could have done a lot better. "Wait, what was the party you were going to?"

"There was no party, not really." He folded his hands in front of himself. "It was supposed to be a hookup I found online."

"You have to be careful with that."

"I know."

"Was this better?" Guiding his hands apart, I slipped mine around his waist, moving close so our dicks just barely touched again. His twitched in response, and mine replied.

"Much." He considered me with those green eyes and leaned to kiss me lightly.

"If it weren't two in the morning, I'd offer you a full-service deflowering, Bennet. Let's shower and get to bed."

He didn't move as I reached to turn on the water.

"What's involved in the full service?" He bit his lower lip.

"Well," I ran my gaze over him and slipped my hand around his lower back again, tugging him close. His erection stabbed against mine. "I'd suck that sweet cock of yours, lick your balls and asshole. Then, how do you think you'd like it? Would you want to fuck me, or me fuck you?"

He took a moment to answer. "I-I don't know."

"Try both ways. I love to top, but I'll open up for the right dick and the right angle. And you, my hot hitchhiker, have a great dick."

Bennet put a hand on my chest and let his gaze drop. "I want to, Arthur. I do, but..." He puffed a loud breath at the ceiling.

I pivoted his gaze back to mine with a hand behind his neck. "What?"

He took a moment to focus fully back on me. "This has been a lot for me. I... Sorry, I'm lame."

Holding his face by the cheeks, I could hardly imagine a more adorable reaction. Not adorable; that's condescending. I'd been in his place once and would have appreciated a more gentle hand guiding me then. "No, you're right. We can save that for later. For now, shower, bed, breakfast, and we'll take care of your car."

# God Cock

You know a relationship has gone stale when you're topping and fake your orgasm. You might say, "What? No, Vic. Guys can't fake their orgasm." Well, good for you for apparently never having to do it. You can if you moan and grunt enough. Flex your dick as you do it. If you know your tells and believe in your acting chops to fool him. So when I noticed my mind wander as I was balls deep in Trev, I knew I had to finish quickly. He came, clenching down on my dick in all the ways that would usually drive me wild, but all I could think about was that pile of laundry nearly overflowing the bin across the room.

Was I over the relationship, or was I not in the mood that night? A week later, it was Thursday again, our night for sex. Trev pushed my book aside, rolling onto me, shoving his tongue into my mouth, licking and slobbering his way down to suck my cock. Hot, I know. Not really suck it, but just move it in and out of his mouth. He moaned and made all the wet noises with the enthusiasm of a teenager who learned everything from a pamphlet about cocksucking. I was the first guy he dated, but I was close to suggesting an open relationship. Not for me. I was busy enough, but for him, for him to go into the world and return with experience. What if I lost him to someone else? It might be worth the risk.

He worked his way back up, his rock-hard cock stabbing into my scrotum. "What's wrong, baby?"

My dick hadn't stirred. It may as well have been thinking about my mother naked on a cold day. I also hated how he called me "baby." He was eight years my junior.

"Sorry, I just had a long day at work." Yeah, I know it's a lie. I work in the children's section of the library. My job is organizing crayons and reading books to field trippers. It's hard to have a bad or long day.

Trev knew it was a lie, too.

"Oh." He rolled off me.

"If you want to..." I made the universal jerk-off hand gesture. "Go ahead." Not that he needed my permission to jerk it, but he'd gotten upset a month after he moved in when he caught me with myself. That was almost a year ago and still our only fight.

He was looking away from me and, after a minute, slipped out of bed and into the bathroom, shutting the door behind him. That alone was a red flag. We never closed doors unless we had company staying over.

I looked between my book and the closed door. Trev was a lot sometimes. An astounding amount of drama can be packed into a twenty-three-year-old body. He was the smartest person I knew, a genius behind the computer screen. But also, fuck, he was nice to look at. An absolutely perfectly sculpted dick on a body that hadn't given up its teenage metabolism yet. He had the kindest smile and was great with the kids when he visited me at work, which he did often, bringing me and the kids treats from his mom's bakery.

All that, but a terrible lay.

I loved everything about him and knew he was the best person I'd ever dated, worth every scrap of my love, but the sex? Three out of ten on a good night, and at his age, I'm sure he wanted it a lot more often than we scheduled it.

I swung from bed, an unintended sigh slipping from my lips as I did.

"Trev, you okay?" I asked with my head resting on the bathroom door frame.

The door snapped open, and Trev strode by me, head held high, never meeting my eye, as he grabbed his pillow and phone. "I'm sleeping in the guest room tonight."

He didn't need to say it. Where else would he be going naked with his pillow and phone at almost midnight on a Thursday? I watched his bare ass disappear into the next room. Cursing, I slipped back into bed. I knew I had some of the blame here, maybe even most of the blame. I plucked him from a bar when he was barely twenty-one. How could I be the slightest bit upset that he lacked the experience he'd be out there gathering if he wasn't at home with me, ordering take-out twice a week and going to Costco on the weekends? You would hardly believe how lame I felt grabbing my phone off the charger and Googling, "How to get better at gay sex." Between all the links to articles about how to top or bottom was an event link, "Exploring the male form, guided self-pleasure."

I tapped it.

There wasn't much information. Just one picture of the instructor, an artsy black and white photo of a thirty-something guy wearing a wool beanie, and nothing else. It was this weekend, a half-hour drive away, promising a reconnection to the body through the exploration of sexual energy. Couples welcome. Sixty-five dollars each.

I bought two tickets.

It wasn't having Trev fuck around to widen his arsenal of sex skills, but it was a step. Hell, I'd been fucking and sucking for fifteen years, but that doesn't mean there wasn't something new for me to learn.

I told Trev the next day that I signed us up for a couple's retreat, leaving it at that. He wanted to know more, but I feigned flirty mystery. It wasn't until I said it out loud that I wondered about the format of this thing. Would we have a private room with quiet spa music, aromatherapy aerosols, and a videotape of the guy in the beanie? What if this was a private session with the beanie guy? I'd strip in front of a stranger for a chance to repair things with Trev and he could barely keep his shirt on at the clubs when we met, so he'd probably be fine. We weren't perfect, but he was the best I'd been with and worth working for. Friday night, he was back in bed, being the little spoon.

"Some retreat," Trev chuckled as I pulled into the strip mall. Bareside Yoga was one of the few shops still in business, sandwiched between a thrift store and a dollar store. "We're doing a yoga class?"

"Not really. It's a guided meditation thing that runs out of here monthly." I'd found a little more in my searching, but still couldn't tell if we'd be in a room alone or what.

The lobby was like any yoga studio in the mid-west, selling candles, oils, CDs with an hour of Nepali singing bowls, though who still owns anything that could play a CD? The man behind the counter, wearing an alpaca poncho and no shoes, greeted us with a bow, hands at heart-center.

"Are you checking in?" he asked gently, though his Boston accent came through strong.

"Yes, Vic Fermi." I showed him the QR code from my email.

"Very good." He checked my name off a list I couldn't read but saw enough to know we weren't alone. "Your session is starting soon, but please stay after, and I can give you a tour." He waved for us to follow him through the doorway into a square room with a recovered wood bench through the middle and lockers lining the walls, beaded bracelets hanging from the keys in the locks. "If you need to use the restroom, they are through the yellow door. Otherwise, please disrobe and be comfortable in the studio." He waved to another door, dim within, spilling that gentle spa music I expected.

We thanked him, and Trev turned to me the second the receptionist pulled a heavy curtain, closing out the light from the lobby.

"Disrobe? Vic, what the fuck is this?"

It was pointless to misdirect with a whimsical mystery at this point. "I think you know as much as I do at this point. I just found the link, thought it looked unique and—"

The curtain parted for a jaw-dropping slice of thick-cut man who could have been Jason Moama's stunt double. Gorgeous long, curly hair, a chest ready to pop the buttons from his shirt... He nodded at us, then crossed the room, quickly pulling off one article of clothing at a time, neatly folding each and stacking them in the bottom of a locker. We both jerked our gaze to his eyes when he turned back to us. "Better hurry up, chaps." His light British accent made it all a little sexier, along with his thighs that could crush a watermelon and his limp cock hanging halfway to his knee.

"Well." Trev cleared his throat. "You've already paid, and we're already here. We may as well see what's going on."

I wasn't so sure I wanted that hot Brit to see my dick, but Trev already had his shirt off. Pushing the key bracelet on, I followed him naked into the studio.

Tan towels were arranged in neat rows, and a dozen pairs of eyes glanced up as we entered. Men from twenty to sixty sat cross-legged, facing the front, ready for this guided mediation. Toward the middle of the room, two towels, the only empty ones, were a little closer to each other than most of the others. Now that I noticed that, I pointed out three other couples in the room. Jason Moama was, blessedly, in the back.

It took everything I could to keep my eyes from wandering as we cut through the crowd to our place. A room full of men without shame or modesty, and I envied every one of them for it.

Trev leaned toward me when we sat. "God-damn, Vic. Who knew this was a thing?" He picked up the small jar of coconut oil at the head of our towels, raising an eyebrow at me.

Beanie Guy entered to soft applause. Fully nude like the rest of us, I felt some small solace that he wasn't hugely endowed or had abs for days. He could have been any guy off the street, just with a powerful air of confidence. He nod-ded thanks. "We have a few newcomers with us today." All eyes turned to Trev and me for just a moment. After a smattering of applause and "welcome"s, the attention returned to Beanie Guy.

He kneeled on the towel in front, resting back on his heels. "Though we practice in the compa-ny of like-mindedness, our practice is our own." His gentle words were spoken in a practiced rhythm. "As every individual's goals vary, so too do our attainments. Draw energy from the bared spirits around you and return that energy twicefold."

I understood his jargon as, "If you cum, that's fine. Feel free to watch the other guys jerk off, so long as they can watch you." Really, what the fuck did I get us into?

"We start in a seat. Pull your heel to press against your perineum."

I followed along, trying to ignore how I was already halfway erect. Trev was fully hard. The Hispanic guy to my right with a shaved head and a fully hard uncut cock. His eyes looked unfocused, letting his mind drift with the slow, deep breathing exercise. The breathing accelerated, using our bellies to draw the air. Beanie Guy moved us back to kneeling and called for the use of the coconut oil. We massaged our scrotums, rubbing thumbs around our balls, stroking only upward, drawing energy from our balls up to our abdomens. I didn't get the spiritual part of the exercise, but I caught the electric thrill of being in a room full of men doing the same.

He invited couples to come together, one behind the other, pulling that sexual energy from the sacral chakra upward to their nipples. I moved behind Trev. The other couples were doing the same, though I noticed one split to each go with a neighbor. Other men were pairing up, leaving only a few alone. It felt orchestrated, as though they'd all decided on their matchups before Trev and I walked into the room. Or maybe they moved with silent tells too subtle for me to notice.

My hands, slick with coconut oil, slid under Trev's balls, across his anus, pressing at a spot just in front. My cock quivered between his legs, a quarter of an inch away, but I ignored it. This moment was for Trev. I massaged against his perineum, feeling the root of his erection just under the skin. Beanie Guy's words blended into the spa music, but I sensed his urging. Move across your body, draw the energy forming at that point, shift it to spread and fill you.

I rubbed and stretched the skin of his scrotum as Trev breathed slow and deep, his hands back on my hips. I pulled the energy up to his waiting cock. I'd never felt him that hard before. My every urge was to stroke him to completion, but no. Why cum from your dick when you could cum from your whole body? Spread and disperse that sexual power. Pushing his cock hard against his belly, I stroked up to his ribs, then started it again, tickling his anus, across the space between his balls, across his dick, and up.

"You do not have a cock," whispered Beanie Guy. He was close, breath tickling my ear. "You are a cock. A God Cock. Do you feel it?"

"I feel it," I breathed into Trev's neck. "You're a God Cock." The words meant nothing but felt absolutely right.

Trev reached between his legs, guiding my coconut-oiled dick to his anus, pressing back against me. I let him, entering just enough to pressure his prostate while starting the ritual again, pulling divine God Cock energy from behind his balls up to spread through his body.

That wasn't enough for him as he shifted his hips back, exhaling a long breath while effortlessly slipping around me without hesitation, pressing against me like he hoped I could give him more. His fingers dug into my thighs as I pushed, not thrusting, but with the sensation that I bore deeper into him.

Never before had I felt so connected. His energy broke all barriers, rushing through his back and my chest pressed against it. It soared through my veins to my cock and overpowered me in a breath. The circle complete, I came hard, pumping just a few inches into him, spilling onto the tan towel. It overcame him at the same moment, arcing shots up his chest, almost hitting his chin.

Slipping from him, he grabbed the edge of the towel to wipe his chest, belly, and ass before the cum could run.

The moment pulled away, returning to a reality with the dozen other men around us. We were not alone in getting caught up in the God Cock energy. Another couple was cleaning up, two others were going through the exercise while locking eyes with the other, three men were sucking each other in a ring in the corner, and Jason Moama's stunt double was on his back getting plowed by an older Asian gentleman. There were a few empty towels, as well.

Beanie Guy squatted beside us, letting his dick hang heavy with his legs wide, smiling with a hand on each of our knees. "It pleases me to see you have found your energy today. You may stay as long as you wish, and please, return to us at any time." He raised his dry, calloused hands to cup our cheeks, looking at us one at a time with an intense emerald stare. I thought for a breath that he might lean to kiss us, which I might not have objected to. He stood, letting his gaze linger on us again before turning to the man next to us, going through his exercise of drawing the energy upward, his eyes closed tight. Beanie Guy stepped behind him, squatting to whisper in the man's ear. He came a breath later, shooting a stream to the head of his towel, then fell forward to his hands.

Now that we were this far into it, I wanted to stay and watch how everyone finished, but Trev was up and pulling me with him.

"Fucking hell, Vic. I've never cum that hard." He snagged a fresh towel from a pile beside the lockers and again wiped off his belly and ass. I took one to clean up the coconut oil as best I could.

Dressed again, the alpaca poncho man tried to sell us yoga packages, but we got away with just a few pamphlets and a class schedule.

"That was a bunch of crap about God Cock energy," Trev started saying in the car. "Do we have any coconut oil at home?"

It wasn't a bunch of crap. I felt it, or at least felt something right at the end. Trev's energy flowed through me, blasting its way to complete our circuit. It wasn't about sex, fucking, putting my dick in him. It was the connection, the compatibility, that allowed him to flow through unimpeded.

In that instant, as I waited for traffic to clear so I could turn out of the run-down shopping plaza, I knew I would do anything to keep Trev in my life.

# Night of the Storm

I WOKE TO FIREWORKS. No, not fireworks. Nearly continuous lightning and a constant, low rumble of thunder. I'd never seen anything like it, flashing a strobe against the horizontal blinds. I sat up on my elbows and tossed the sweaty sheets aside. The air never worked well in the dorms, and ours had been completely busted for over a month.

Two feet from the end of my twin-long bed was the side of my roommate's. After a year and a half of sleeping in the same room as him, it never ceased to surprise me how Brian could sleep through anything. Now that I was awake, there was no way I'd fall back asleep with the light show in our bedroom. Feet on the floor, I glanced at Brian laid out on his bed, sheets tangled around his legs, knees spread, his t-shirt riding high to expose his belly, and the trail of hair disappearing into his boxers. I sighed deeply, fantasizing for the thousandth time what it would be like to run my fingers across his skin under that elastic. My hand found the growing bulge in my boxers as I thought about it.

No. Stop.

Brian's my roommate, my friend. He's straight.

I'm pretty sure he's straight. We'd never specifically discussed it, but that's the default, yeah? Not discussing it didn't keep me from being gay.

Fuck.

I stood and left the bedroom. The sliding door to the balcony in the living room looked out over the tops of trees and a sky shuddering with a low grumble of lightning. My hand found my cock again, easily fumbling it through the fly in my boxers. I was rock hard, ready to blow, though I'd barely touched myself. Oh, the joys of being nineteen.

Fuck. Just do it. Maybe I could get back to sleep.

With a wad of tissues in the other hand, it only took a few strokes before I felt the tension build. I couldn't stop myself from glancing back at the bedroom door, half hoping Brian would walk out at just that moment. Would he avert his eyes, embarrassed, and flee to the bathroom? Maybe he'd stare at me, debating what to do, before slipping his dick free and joining me?

That was enough.

I gasped, my cum filling the wadded tissue, leaking through and onto my hand. I leaned my forehead against the cool glass until the last spasm had faded.

This couldn't last forever, holding in these fantasies, but neither could I act on them.

When I turned off the bathroom light behind me, the lightning storm had yet to lose its intensity, still splashing a near-solid wash of light over sleeping Brian. He had one hand across his chest and the other on his thigh. My dick stirred again.

Sitting on the edge of my bed, I watched the hand on his thigh slide higher, slipping under his boxers. The fabric bulged and shifted. I'd seen Brian in his boxers plenty in our time living together, but never able to study the scene. I called myself a pervert for looking, but neither did I look away. I didn't stop myself as I stood, walking around the end of my bed to look down at him. What would he think if he opened his eyes now? As I reached trembling fingers to within an inch of his, to lightly brush the outline of his growing erection? His boxers were the cheap kind with no button on the fly that spread wide when you spread your legs, just like his legs were at that moment. I could slip a finger in, touch his dick. Stroke a finger down his length. He could sleep through anything.

Without warning, I came again. Luckily, my boxers caught it.

Goddammit. This is perverted. I'm a pervert.

I rushed around the other side of my bed to fish a clean pair of boxers from my dresser. Unless I rolled over my bed, I'd have to pass Brian on my way to the bathroom. I...

I glanced back at him. His hand had moved again, now around his shaft, bursting from the loose fly. His thumb curled around the base, while his fingers cupped his balls. A year and a half of quietly pining over the man, and there was his dick, right there on display, backlit by a constant flash of heat lightning. Uncircumcised, maybe a little longer than mine. I'd never touched another man's dick. At that moment, I wanted nothing but to touch Brian's cock. He could sleep through anything. Maybe I could stroke it? With my tongue.

Somehow, my dick, slick and sticky with its last load, responded in full.

I shifted to the end of my bed, wanting to sear everything about this moment into my memory. My right hand went down my boxers, to grasp my own as I ran one finger up his length, my arm tingling with the smooth texture, the firmness just under the surface.

Brian shifted.

I fled.

"You okay?" he called after as I got to the doorway, his words laced with drowsiness. "Oh, shit."

"Yeah, I..." I turned back, keeping my clean boxers waded behind me. He was adjusting himself, probably shoving his dick away. "I couldn't sleep, with the storm."

"Huh." He stared at the blinds for a moment. "It really something out there," he said quietly. "I just had a weird dream."

"Yeah?" I moved back to sit on the edge of my bed.

"Yeah, I," he laughed, sitting up and swinging his feet to the floor. He ran a hand through his thick, dark hair. "You were in it."

If this was a trap, if he knew what I had just done to him, he didn't seem mad about it.

"We had a girl over, getting ready to..." He twirled his hand. It was cute and a little reassuring to see him as unsure about sex as I. "Then she just up and left."

I waited a few breaths for him to continue, but he didn't. "Well, that was rude of her."

"So you finished us both off." The words spilled from him.

"How considerate of me," I tried to laugh.

He stared at me for another long breath. One hand went to his lap to squeeze and adjust. I couldn't hold back the tiny gasp.

"I woke up hard as ever." With the light behind him, I couldn't make out the exact movements of his hand in his lap, but I watched his shoulder move rhythmically. "You want to, Z?"

"Want to...?" I let the question hang. Maybe I wanted to hear him say specifics.

"It'll be our secret." He spread his knees.

I couldn't resist, couldn't say no. Like a doomed sailor drawn to the siren, I wiped my sticky right hand on my clean boxers and left them on the bed as I crossed the four feet. Stopping by his knees, he looked up at me with a grin. That grin that often made me want to do more than see him naked, but to kiss him, hold him...

"What should I do?" I asked.

He took my left hand in his, guiding it down to glance his erection. "Do like in the videos I know you watch."

I froze. Fuck. He'd seen my browser history. How long had he known?

My thoughts left just as quickly as he pressed my hand more firmly against him. My palm slipped around his shaft, thumb toward his belly, stroking and applying pressure as I thought I might like it. He moaned and leaned back on his palms. He liked it, too. His foreskin made it easier to work, pulling on him.

But I wanted more.

My dick screamed for attention, but I ignored it. It had done enough already. I dropped to my knees, my mouth a few inches from Brian's cock. This close, I could smell him. Before that instant in my life, I would have cringed at the scent, musk and sweat, but now it only drove me closer to a third cumming.

Still stroking, I ran my tongue up his length, and he gasped again. Pulling back his foreskin, I licked his crown, lapping up the precum spread across it.

"Fuck!"

He tried to pull back, but his load hit me on the cheek, on my ear.

I came for the third time that night. I'd ache tomorrow.

"Sorry," Brian sputtered, using his hands to find his cum in the dark.

I wiped a finger across my cheek to my mouth, tasting him as I stood.

"This stays between us," he said, though it might have been a question.

Who would I tell? "Yeah."

"I'll clean this up in the morning. Good night, Z." He was back in bed, sheets tucked to his ribs, and rolled toward the wall, toward the window. Sometime during our encounter, the lightning had stopped.

I grabbed another new pair of boxers and rushed to the bathroom to clean up. His cum had gotten in my hair. He didn't shift when I climbed back into my bed.

By the time I woke, Brian had slipped off to his morning classes and was still gone when I returned from mine. I came out of our bathroom mid-afternoon to him standing in the middle of the living room, hands clasped in front of him.

"About last night," he started.

"I won't tell anyone."

He stepped forward, halving the distance between us. "Want to do it again?" He unzipped his jeans. His meaning was clear. "I'll try to last longer."

I dropped to my knees, unbelting and pulling his jeans to his ankles. His cock was already at full attention as I pulled down his boxers, taking in the full sight of his member only inches from my nose. The soft fluff of his pubes, how his balls hung low but tucked up as I started to work him. Pulling back his foreskin, I took him fully in my mouth until he threatened to gag me. I looked up, my mouth full, but his gaze was on the ceiling, lips parted in a gasping moan.

He lasted a little longer than the night before and tried to pull out as he came, hitting me across the lips and neck, as well as the couch behind me.

I stood, hand down my pants, ready to burst. I wanted to kiss him, tell him how many times I've thought about us becoming exactly this.

"Thanks," he said, moving past me and closing the bathroom door behind him without a glance.

Balls aching, I stared at that closed door, realizing our relationship had changed, but not how I'd hoped.

I wouldn't be standing here with my limp dick in my hands when he finally came out. I quickly put on my shoes and fled. Finding the familiar path through the forest behind the dorms, my mind churned with what had happened. Brian has known I'm gay. He'd seen my search history and known I'd want to pleasure him. I'd taken his bait and thrown out a year and a half of friendship to suck dick twice.

No. He consented. At least once he woke up, he consented. It was his idea. Maybe he rushed to the bathroom as he tried to accept the truth that I did three years ago. One that I never told anyone, but he knew? Wouldn't that be great if two gay boys were put in the same dorm room?

The path led me back to the dorms, a complete circuit beaten out by decades of students with energy to burn. How many had fucked out here? How thrilling would that be to suck off Brian in the woods, where anyone could stumble upon us?

I was hard again when I unlocked the dorm room. There was no sign of Brian, though I knew he had no more classes today. Whatever. We'd deal with this eventually when he got home, or maybe we never would. We'd ignore each other until the semester ended, and we could pick a new room. Or he'd regularly pull out his dick for me to service. I would, happily and greedily, but we'd never discuss it.

I was in the shower, doing all I could not to sit down and hug my knees, when I felt the slight change in pressure as the curtain billowed outward.

"Brian?"

"Hey," he said. I heard the door click behind him. "Sorry about earlier."

"Sorry you got cum on the couch or sorry you ran off?" I tried to laugh, but it came out as a weak chuckle. My sense of vulnerability spiked when his shadow came across the sheer curtain.

He was quiet for a long moment. I stood in the hot water, watching him shift.

"Can I join you?" he finally asked. His shadow came into focus as he reached for the curtain, shifting it aside before I could answer. As he stepped in beside me, I saw something I hadn't seen yet: his flaccid cock, though that quickly changed.

"Brian, I—"

He cut off my words with his lips locking onto mine. His hands gripped my hips, crushing us together. His cock stabbed into my belly while his hands slid up my back carefully, tenderly.

"I'm sorry we waited so long to do that," he said when he finally pulled back, pressing his forehead into mine. "I've wanted you since I first saw you, Z, but my parents would kill me if they knew."

"So don't tell them." My hands explored across his back, pulling him closer into the water.

"Let me do something." He gently pressed my shoulders to turn me around. He grasped my cock at the base, slowly sliding to the tip and back while his raging hard cock ground against my ass.

That would come later.

"This is how I do myself," he breathed into my ear. I leaned my head back into him as one hand reached back to hold him against me. Despite that, he moved his hips, sliding his dick over my hole.

He sped up his pace, and my knees weakened as I came. He kept one hand on my dick, still slowly stroking, and used the other to shift my head to kiss him.

When he finally stopped, I turned to him without increasing the distance. My eyes flicked down.

"Want me to...?"

"I don't think I'll say no."

It didn't take long, with the water streaming through my hair, him holding onto my head with both hands. When he was about to blow, he tried slipping out, but I gripped his ass tight, holding him in me to shoot down my throat.

When I stood, he ran his tongue across my lips before kissing me again. "You better not make my grades drop, Z." He grinned that grin that always made me want to kiss him—this time, I did.

# The Sales King

MISTER DUPIN TOLD ME this conference would change everything and I would never doubt his word. Why else would I be wedged beside him on a Greyhound for six states?

Well, there was the other reason. His tight slacks didn't leave much to the imagination, and despite his insistence that we would spend the whole bus ride perfecting our presentation for the AquaVacc, he was now half reclined, arms crossed against his tight Oxford, dozing. The man was a sales genius. He could doze if he needed to. We'd prepare when we got to the motel tonight.

The bus hit a bump, and Mister Dupin stirred just enough to shift in his seat, and I looked him over. Those long lashes, perfectly parted hair just long enough to cover his ears. If he opened his eyes, I'd see that steely gray that I fell into when I started working for him three years ago. He deserved his rest. He shifted his hips, drawing my attention to the bulge growing along his hip bone in the tight slacks. I might have drooled a bit at the sight of such a thick cock. I'd heard from everyone around the office that it was a regular tool for the sales king in sealing a deal and wondered, with a flare of jealousy, who would get that cock at the conference.

Mine responded, tight in my jeans, making me feel a little lightheaded. The bus was mostly empty. The seats across the aisle were empty. Fuck it. I reclined to match Mister Dupin and slipped my right hand down my pants, feeling the wetness of my precum against the back of my hand as I wrapped my fingers around my cock, squeezing one finger at a time in a languid rhythm. With the other hand, I traced my fingers down the length of that bulge in Mister Dupin's slacks from hip to crotch. Fuck, he was big. What was he dreaming about to get so hard? How many lucky people would get this cock over the weekend to finalize a sale? The AquaVacc line was built on his fat cock in an unspoken agreement and understanding. Competitors would throw in promotional wares or expedited shipping. AquaVacc had a ten-inch dick and skilled hips. A ten-inch dick, just a thin layer of wool away from my fingers. I'd buy three AquaVaccs to have this in my mouth—four for my ass. Shit, I'd buy one just to see it.

I craned back, looking over the seats and the few other dozing riders illuminated by the regular flashes of streetlamps on the highway. My cock throbbed in my hand, aching for release. I debated doing it right there with a hand stroking that amazing salesman's dick. It would be fully dark when we got to the motel. I could disappear into my room before Mister Dupin noticed the sticky, wet stain.

No, I didn't pack enough to waste clothes by filling them with cum.

I stood, rushing to the little stall bathroom, closing the door behind me with a click. I couldn't get my pants down quickly enough, meeting my gaze in the tiny mirror lit by a red bulb overhead.

"You're going to make so many sales," I told the reflection.

"He's going to give you that dick as a thank you." I grabbed for a wad of cheap toilet tissue with my off hand, furiously stroking with the other.

"He's going to pound that fat cock so deep up your ass that you'll taste his cum."

My reflection pinched and gasped with an explosion deep in my hips. I rested my forehead against it, letting the last spasms quiet. Dropping the heavy tissue into the toilet, I knew there was no way I wasn't leaving a mess on the floor or the sink, but I couldn't care about that. We'd be at the motel in an hour, and it's not like they'd track down who came all over in a bus bathroom. That's probably why there was just one red bulb, to hide all the other sins.

When I stepped out, a single reading light was on ahead over Mister Dupin. He looked up from a product catalog as I slid back into my seat, flashing a grin.

"Sorry, Will. I think I slept this whole ride. Buses do that to me and always have. Did you get any rest?"

I bit my lip and shook my head.

"That's okay. I think we have our presentation down well enough. Maybe we could cram in a few minutes when we get to the hotel and work on our rhythm."

Fucking yes, please. "Good idea, Mister Dupin."

He laughed, running a hand through that perfect hair. "We're in this together this weekend, Will. Call me Randy. Are you ready to change the future of home cleaning?"

"Yes, sir. I mean... yes." I tried to match his enthusiasm.

"That's what I want to hear, Will."

Mister Dupin stormed out of the motel office to where I stood surrounded by our luggage and packaged presentation materials in the damp parking lot.

"They said we were too late and gave away one of our rooms. This is a single full," he huffed. "They're going to send a cot. I'll take that. I'm sorry, Will, this is your first big conference, and it's already off to a bad start."

"That's okay Mister... Randy. We'll make the most of it." A wild, deviant idea came to me. "We can share the bed, I'm sure. Maybe we'll be a better team tomorrow if our brainwaves synch up as we sleep."

He chuckled. "That's why I like you, Will. You'll go far with out-there thinking. Let me help you with all that." He started gathering luggage under his strong arms.

The tiny room reeking of antiseptic cleaners barely fit our luggage and presentation materials. Mister Dupin... Randy pulled out posterboards with charts and bulleted lists for us to practice. A half-hour later, there was a single knock at the door. Outside, they'd left a cot folded in half on rollers. After ten minutes of trying to get it through the door and around our luggage, Randy sighed and tossed up his hands.

"I guess we're bunking together," he said, eyeing the bed with a worn duvet exactly like what my grandmother would have in her guest room. "Do you have a preference on the side? I'm versatile."

I pointed to the side closer to the wall.

"Great. I'm going to hit it, then. I slept the whole way here, but you can't have enough rest for what's coming tomorrow." He clapped me on the shoulder as he took a smaller bag from our luggage and disappeared into the bathroom.

I hadn't packed pajamas. I slept naked at home and was supposed to have my own room here. Though... I pulled back the sheets, inspecting for bedbugs.

I felt woefully unprepared for so much of this weekend when the bathroom door opened

again. Randy wore pinstriped, buttoned pajamas. He dropped his toiletry pack with the rest
of the luggage and jerked a thumb at the bathroom. "All yours, tiger." He winked.

My reflection stared back as I brushed my
teeth. What would my part be when Randy
brought a potential client back tomorrow night?
Would he bring them to a shithole motel like
this? Surely not. But where else? The HomePure
Innovations Expo had every place at or near
capacity for ten miles.

"Forget your pajamas?" Randy asked with a
chuckle. The room was dark except for the
reading light on his nightstand. He sat against
the headboard, holding that same product catalog from before.

Looking down at my jeans and polo, I tried
to match his good humor. "I thought I'd packed
everything. I must have forgotten nightclothes
in my excitement."

"I always keep a 'go bag' packed so I never
worry about forgetting the important things.
Always be prepared."

I couldn't tell if that was an admonishment of
my lack of preparedness or simple advice.

"To be honest with you, Will, this is more than
I usually sleep in." He took off his reading glass-

es, setting them on the nightstand. "Honestly, Will, anything you need to sleep well tonight. It'll be a long day. You can't sleep in Wranglers." He flicked the top button of his silk pinstripes.

Swallowing hard, I unbuttoned and tugged off my jeans. His eyes never moved from me as I approached the other side of the bed in my polo and boxers, sliding in beside him.

I stared into those steely gray eyes so close to my own for just a breath before ripping off my polo, tossing it over the end of the bed, and scooting down to lay my head on the pillow, sheets tucked to my chin.

"Do you mind if I..." Holding that top button, he flapped his pajamas.

"Not at all."

"Thanks, Will." He kept his eyes locked on mine as he popped each button, only looking away when he pulled the long sleeve shirt back over his broad shoulders. For a man who worked as much as he did, Randy's body was like a chiseled Greek god's. He had the hairy chest of a Sears model and thick arms corded with muscle. Tossing his shirt off the side of the bed, he reached to flick off the light, leaving us in total darkness while my eyes adjusted. Even at the edge of the bed, I felt him move against me, scooting down, then raising his hips to slide off at least his pinstripe pants.

"That's better," he sighed.

His body heat seared against me. I could feel his leg hairs brush mine and I wasn't sure what to do with my hands, so folded them across my stomach.

"Good night, Will. We're going to have a great day tomorrow. We'll change the future of home cleaning."

"Good night, Randy."

He rolled away from me, shaking the bed with every tiny movement until his back gently touched my shoulder with every breath. I let my arm fall between us, my wrist against his bare ass. My cock screamed for attention, and I finally gave it some, gently squeezing, while I lay there fantasizing about Randy Dupin, a god amongst mortals in the world of vacuum cleaner sales. I listened to the diety's slow, deep breathing; I was burned by his warmth against me. In my mind, he rolled to his other side, cock falling into my hand between us. That was the start of half my scenarios.

I woke to the woosh of the bathroom door opening. The bed was empty beside me, sheets and duvet folded neatly to the pillow. Sitting up, leaning back on my elbow, Randy stepped from around the corner to the bathroom, bare to the cheap white towel wrapped low around his waist. He was combing his hair and flashed me a grin.

"About time, sleepy head." He patted my foot through the sheets. "Your turn. We'll have just enough time to hit that little diner I saw off the highway."

He turned to the pile of luggage, back muscles tensing as he dug through to find the one he wanted.

"Could you hand me that?" I asked, pointing to my tan canvas bag.

Randy glanced back, then followed my gesture, leaning over the stack. His towel came loose as he straightened, but he caught it before exposing his front. As casual as a pro athlete, he whipped the towel back in place, not caring that he flashed everything at me in doing it.

Canvas bag over my steepled boxers, I fled to the bathroom.

A wave of professionalism hit me when I stepped into the cold water. This was a weekend to learn from a master, to solidify my place in his empire. If he saw me as some sex-crazed kid, I'd be back in the mailroom. No, I had to make today perfect. We would sell the Aqua-Vacc. I would be the model assistant. If he needed me to catch a movie while he sealed a deal with that dick, I'd do it without question. Still, I couldn't help but feel jealous of this imaginary person with his balls slapping against them. I turned the water colder, refusing to give my dick the attention it wanted. It could wait until after a successful day of sales.

And successful it was. We'd hoped to sell the AquaVacc to a local motel chain, but now the owner of a multi-million dollar regional franchise sat at the table littered with two dozen empty beer bottles. He probably wasn't much older than me but was used to existing on his daddy's money. He had barely taken his eyes off Randy since we left the convention center nine beers and three shots of whiskey ago. He wanted to fuck my boss; he wanted to fuck the man I wanted to fuck me. I didn't see him as competition, though. No, this rich cunt would pave the way for me.

This kid, Cliffton was his name, would slide closer to Randy, maybe put a hand on his thigh, while my boss kept prying him for order assurances. For every stitch his hand moved closer to Randy's groin along those tight wool slacks, he promised another thousand units sold, repair contracts, and cleaning supply budgets. By the time Cliffton's fingers brushed the tip of Randy's groin, he'd promised a twenty-three million dollar contract over the next ten years. My boss never took his hands off the beer bottle on the table before him.

I'd felt Randy up on the bus for free yesterday. I didn't even feel shame or regret about it.

"I'll send the paperwork Monday," Randy said, scooting from the booth. He handed me my jacket and pulled on his own. "I'm looking forward to a long and productive relationship." He couldn't have sounded more professional, not the man I'd watched get felt up the last hour.

Cliffton staggered from the booth to shake Randy's hand. With a gesture so smooth, anyone across the bar would miss it, Randy grabbed Cliffton's crotch. He winked and released just as quickly. I shook the stunned man's hand and jogged after Randy lighting two cigarettes in the parking lot.

"That was amazing!" I accepted the smoke with a deep draw. "I thought he was going to come back with us," I spoke before I thought.

Perhaps it was the whiskey speaking, and I laughed at myself.

"The key is to leave them wanting more, Will. If we'd shaken and left, he would feigned amnesia when I call on Monday. Now, by grabbing one kid's dick, we're millionaires. Cliffton will remember that when he's fucking his wife tonight."

"Wait, we?"

"I won't forget your part in this Will." He turned, stumbling toward the road. I caught him under the arm before he fell, looking at me with those steely, though glassy, eyes. "I'm fucked. Let's get back to the hotel. I have a bottle of something special to celebrate." He started walking again, slowly and carefully.

I glanced back at the bar entrance, then tossed away the cigarette as I jogged to catch up to Randy, slipping a hand around his waist to steady him. Or steady myself.

"You're just leaving Cliffton there? I thought you..." Was it just office gossip how he landed each sale?

He scoffed. "I fucked a hundred Clifftons or Harriets but learned you get more giving less. There's a nugget of wisdom for you, Will." He walked his fingers up my chest, cupped my cheek, and then stared at his hand as he opened and closed it slowly. "Fuck, I'm fucked. How did I manage to hold it together that long in there?"

The motel was only a few minutes down the dark road, and Randy seemed a little better by the time I was fumbling for the key. I opened the door, and he fell across the bed.

"You did great today, Will." He pushed to flop to his back, knees hanging wide over the edge. He fumbled with the buttons on his shirt.

"Need help?" I shut the door behind me, tugging at my tie as I crossed to him. Randy bit his lip, looking up at me through his eyelashes and pushing up on his palms. I slid my hand down his chest, carefully unlooping each button, and grabbed a handful of his shirt on either side to untuck it from his pants. Spreading my hands over his hairy, toned chest, I pushed the shirt away and down his arm, feeling every inch of skin as I did. His hand shot out for my belt buckle, efficiently yanking it open, and tugged my belt from its loops.

He leaned back for me to unzip his slacks, and I pressed my hand into his fat cock as I did.

"You want to get that bottle from my bag to celebrate?"

I couldn't imagine what would be a better celebration than this, but I nodded all the same, dropping my shirt on the floor. The world was already taking a moment to catch up when I turned my head. We didn't need another drink.

"Light blue bottle," he said. I glanced back at him, slipping a hand down his pants.

I expected a rare vintage wine or whiskey, but the only blue bottle was four ounces of water-based personal lubricant.

"That's it," said Randy. He raised a single eyebrow, the glassy stare from the bar fading quickly. "Do you want to use that, Will? In here, we're just two men who are set for life. Two men that could quit right now, but we have that drive. We're going to keep moving up. More money, more power. Do you have that drive, Will?"

"I do."

"Show me. Show me your drive."

My fingers found the button on my trousers. I dropped them, tugged my boxers down, and shook my hips to let them fall to the shag carpet. I stepped out of them, wearing only my socks, with a cock like granite pointing directly at him.

His eyes had never wavered from mine as I stripped, but now he let them slowly wash over me, working from my feet up. Randy slid his thumbs into his waistband, lifted his hips, and pushed down his slacks and boxers, letting them fall from the edge of the bed. He pushed to the center, legs spread, one hand around the base of his fat cock sprouting from a dark bush, the other curled to tease his asshole.

"I don't want to leave you wanting more, Will. I want you to have it all. Anything and everything you want. What do you want, Will?"

I couldn't answer, not with a god plucked from the Sears catalog laid out naked and wanting before me.

"Tell me what you want, Will," he repeated.

I put one knee on the bed, then the other, crawling forward, shoving one under each of his legs, bringing my cock close to his. With a hand on either side of his head, I leaned close to his ear, whispering.

"You."

"Take it," he moaned.

Wiping my precum across his puckered hole, I pressed against him, forceful yet gentle enough to just let my head slide in.

He gasped, gripping one hand through my hair and the other around my hip. Pulling back, I tossed the lube aside and spat into my hand, rubbing that down my shaft.

"Do it. Wreck me," he gasped.

I took his massive cock in my hand, stroking it until he let his head fall back. Then I slid mine into him. Not fast or hard, but steady and sure. Like how we could build our own cleaning empire. Each stroke came out almost to the head, then pressed deep until my balls pressed against him. Every deal, we'd see start to completion, nothing rushed, nothing skipped. Once I had it, my hips accelerated, from start to end with every thrust, slamming harder, our bodies slick with sweat.

"Just... like that..." he moaned between thrusts. "Don't break... your pace..." He'd taken over working his cock, using both hands. He pushed his feet into the mattress, arching to put weight on his shoulders.

My balls ached from slapping against him.

The pressure was climaxing, but I didn't break my rhythm, only going harder. My whole body rocked with the first spasm, but still, I kept going, nearly out, then fully in.

"Fuck, that's it!" He dropped his dick to grab my ass and hold me still. The message was clear: he wanted me in him as he...

He tightened around my dick and shot a thick stream across his chest. Then another. Two more. I pressed tight against him with each shot.

Slick with sweat, I pushed my forehead against his, wanting little more at that moment than to kiss him while I felt the last aftershock tightening his sphincter.

"Shit, Will." His breath brushed my cheek, and he gasped lightly as I slid out. "Did you get what you want?"

"Not yet."

I pushed forward onto him, barely noticing his cum smearing across my chest and belly as I kissed him, tongue pushing between his lips, hands interlocking with his, holding them over his head. He struggled against me, slow and without the power I knew him capable of. He liked this. Randy Dupin, sales god of vacuum cleaners, wanted to be controlled, wanted to be fucked.

I could do that. I'd gladly do that. What Cliffton signed a ten-year contract to trace a finger along; I'd use both hands to stroke to comple-

tion. I'd swallow that load without a drop wasted. I'd fuck him to oblivion every night, three
times a day, if it honed his divine-given powers.

Randy Dupin, the sales god of vacuum cleaners, the man I'd worshipped for three years,
was my sex slave.

# Mtop89

YOU WANT TO KNOW how I met him? Okay. It was at the gym. At least, that's what I tell everyone.

I was on the stair climber, level eleven, when a notification chirped in my earbuds.

> Mtop89: hey

His profile said he was less than thirty feet away, and he was, on the treadmill six machines to my left. I watched him watching me for a moment before replying.

> Otter19: hey.

> Mtop89: i haven't seen you here before

His use of "you" rather than "u" tugged at my heart momentarily.

> Otter19: just in town visiting.

He slowed his machine to a cool-down walk, stretching his hands behind his head and twisting to show his biceps. They looked nice. Everything about him did. His loose shorts flopped with every step, making me regret that I didn't get a good look while he moved faster. His tank top clung to a stocky frame of packed muscle.

> Mtop89: how long?

Which route to take? Tell him I was visiting my dad through the weekend or that I'm a seven-inch grower? The gym was nearly empty this late. We'd have the locker room or showers to ourselves.

Fuck. I wanted to see him naked. I wasn't particularly picky at this time in my life, but he was hot. So fucking hot.

> Otter89: want to find out?

I winked at him after he read my message and glanced back at me.

> Mtop89: saucy. i like it

> Otter19: done with your workout?

> Mtop89: i have some left in me

> Otter19: i'm hitting the shower.

His hands were on the treadmill controls when I glanced back as I entered the locker room. He wouldn't get to see me as a grower, as I was hard as ever when I stuffed my clothes into the locker, wrapping a towel around my waist. The water was instantly hot when I stepped into the stream, rushing to get a legitimate cleansing done while hoping to see fingers curl around the curtain.

My soapy hands gripped my cock, stroking it more than needed to get it clean, and one slipped around to tease my asshole. One finger slipped in to the first knuckle. I could have just finished myself and gone back to Dad's, and debated doing just that when the curtain darkened with a shadow. Mtop89 slipped in, pressing his body against mine, jamming his thick cock into my thigh.

I like kissing, even with a shower hookup, but Mtop89 apparently did not. Grabbing my hips, he spun me around, putting his calloused hands on my shoulders, raking his nails down my back and squeezing my ass. Whatever he wanted to do me, let him. A finger slipped up my crack, finding and pressing against my asshole, pushing a soapy knuckle in.

I leaned into the cold tile with a gasp, angling my hips out for him, stepping my feet to the edges of the stall shower.

His tongue flicked across my ass, startling a shiver down to my knees, threatening to weaken them. It flicked again, then again, then focused and pressed, gaining just a bit of entry. He pushed, alternating with long laps up my crack. His breath came hot and rushed against my hole as the steamy water ran down my back into his face. The thought of him slowly drowning while eating my ass sparked a savage thrill, and I dropped a hand to my dick, stroking with his rhythm. He just as quickly pulled my hand away, taking my cock in a firm grip as he stood.

I never looked back. If Mtop89 wanted me to see, he'd turn my head. Right now, I was his vessel.

His other hand aligned his cock to my hole and pressed. I breathed out, relaxing as he filled me, stretching me and pressing against my prostate. I couldn't take more, but I arched my back into him.

He pushed again.

Fuck, that hasn't been all of him?

I held back a whimper and finally let myself breathe when I felt his hips pressing against my ass.

He pulled out, just an inch, then slammed forward, knocking my head against the tile wall. Again and again, he railed against me with short thrusts that bore the weight like a freight train, sending shocks to every joint in my body, weakening me, and threatening to topple me to the stall floor.

His hand was still on my cock, and he worked it root to tip with something verging on violence. With every thrust, my head knocked at the tile, but I put up my forearm to soften the blow. I wouldn't last much longer, not with the waves of paralyzing, agonizing euphoria he wracked through my body. Not with how he worked my cock with such an even rhythm and crushing grip.

He thrust again but didn't pull out. Instead, he pushed somehow deeper inside me, swelling thicker, firing his load beyond where any other man had in my life—filling me from the inside.

That was enough.

He stopped working my cock on my first spasm, cupping his hand around the head to catch what he could as the water poured over us both. His hand pulled back to, I assume, lick my cum from his fingers. Still deep in me, I felt him flex his colossal cock once more, then pull out in one swift motion. I had to brace a hand to the wall to keep from falling to the floor.

The curtain billowed, and Mtop89 was gone.

Not a word said. I wasn't sure I could pick his face out of a police lineup.

My ass ached from what he did, and it would only be worse over the next hours and to-morrow. The locker room was empty when I stepped out of the shower. A notification await-ed me on my phone.

> Mtop89: thank you

What does one say after someone fucks them to oblivion?

> Otter19: yw. thank YOU. i'll feel that tomorrow.

> Mtop89: how long are you in town?

> Otter19: through the weekend.

> Mtop89: same time tomorrow?

Fucking hell. After what he just did, he'd split me in half with a second go. But what a way to go. My thumb hovered over the send arrow before I tapped it.

Otter19: sure.

I could always ghost him. Never show and block him. It would cost me nothing, but maybe I'd be able to sit properly on the train ride home.

Halfway back to Dad's, my phone chirped.

Mtop89: really, thank you

This was getting weird. I read that with the emotion of someone who needed to dick someone deep to get over emotional trauma, even for just a moment of bliss: a scorned lover or a dead goldfish.

Mtop89: dinner?

I could eat, and Dad would be long in bed by now. Was a shower plow turning into a legitimate date?

Otter19: now?

Mtop89: yeah

There was a diner not far from the condo that would be quiet enough at this time to give us privacy but still busy enough to have witnesses in case Mtop89 wanted to murder me.

> Otter19: blue door diner?

This was farther than I went after any hookup.

> Mtop89: brt :)

He was already seated in a corner booth when I walked in. We both ordered breakfast at 11pm. He told me he'd just gotten a big promotion at his marketing job but had no one to celebrate with, having broken up with his long-term partner a month before. Apparently, he hadn't realized how down he was until he was deep in me. Hearing that someone eating your ass might have prevented them from self-harm should be an absolute mood killer, but he brought it back around to suggest we go out dancing. I told him I'm not much of a dancer, and he countered with the dive bar a block over for whiskey shots, followed by making out in his car. That, I could agree to. I did like to kiss, and apparently, Mtop89 did as well.

And that's the true story of how I met my husband. We just celebrated fifteen years. I haven't walked the same since.

# Lighthouse Keeper's Son

"YOU THINK THAT LITTLE ginger's family?"

I gave my husband an exasperated look, then glanced past him at the young twenty-something passing out informational pamphlets about the lighthouse. It was obvious that he was trying to butch up his behavior, and rightly so. Quinn and I had gotten plenty of judging looks as we walked the beaches and streets of this overly conservative vacation spot. Not like we were going to stop holding hands, though. Fuck em.

The kid shook blond hair from his dark eyes, giving Quinn and me another look before returning to pass out his pamphlets. After us, the next youngest in the crowd had twenty years on us, all far more interested in the market stalls selling the collectible home goods you'd expect on grandma's curio cabinets. I suppose it was all grandmas shopping here.

"He said his name was Martin?" Quinn asked.

I grunted an affirmative.

"Well, Martin's got a nice little ass."

I elbowed him and turned my attention fully to the lighthouse before us. We were here for history. Harborview Cove was famous for Civil War landmarks, prohibition rum runners, and white sand beaches. It was also huge for a place to get all the little handmade shit that collects dust around the house, but Quinn and I were always history nerds. We'd already visited two cemeteries since we drove in yesterday.

As such, we were the only two in the crowd of a hundred looking up at the old lighthouse. Perched at the edge of a rugged cliff, its weathered stones stood sentinel over the crashing waves below, whispering of bygone eras. Ivy and moss wound intentionally up the tightly fit masonry, evoking thoughts of a skill not seen in today's construction.

"They're trying to raise money to modernize the light," Quinn summarized the pamphlet. "They want to bring this back into operation, if only for aesthetic value."

I noted the broken glass darkened with the patina of age around where the lamp should be. Restoring the lighthouse would probably just mean running electricity out here and installing the lamp. It wouldn't be hard, but it wouldn't be free.

"Let's take a look." Quinn laced his fingers through mine and led the way up the gravel path. I glanced back at the kid once more, catching him snapping his attention from us.

Yeah, he definitely played for our team.

We circled the lighthouse once, pausing behind it, and wished for a railing on the side overlooking the bluff. There was barely enough space to get a riding lawnmower through without toppling forty feet to the frothing waves below. The view, though, took our breath away. The lighthouse blocked out the chatter of the market, leaving us alone in the shade with only the crash of waves below.

I sauntered to Quinn, slipping a hand around his waist under his tank top. "We could totally make out back here."

He kissed me gently. "We could." Then he twirled us to press me against the cool stone. "Imagine being a lighthouse keeper in 1837, all alone out here. What would you do to pass the time?"

"Probably the same as I do now. Read and jerk off."

"Yeah?" Quinn waggled his eyebrows. "I wonder if we can go inside."

"I don't think they want us to, but I saw the door around the side."

We came into the view of the market below again for just a breath before slipping into the lighthouse through the old, but not original, unlocked door.

The inside was a thirty-foot circle and looked staged for eventual tours. A cot with brown wool blankets, a poorly made bookcase overflowed with antique tomes, a cast iron stove, a tall and broad wardrobe, and a table with a checkers board and deck of cards. Sturdy stairs spiraled up the edge of the room to a ceiling forty feet up, probably the lamp room.

Quinn closed the door behind us and took a deep breath. "Imagine this place stinking of kerosine and a hermit's musk." His words echoed through the hollow structure.

"You can really set a scene. Kerosine and stank. I'm so aroused." My tone dripped with sarcasm, but I was still getting hard. We loved our history, but that didn't stop us from taking our dicks out in the middle of it.

I pushed him back, and a little gasp escaped when the cold stone touched his bare shoulders. My tongue pushed against his, exploring familiar territory, before my lips traced across his cheek, down his neck to his collarbone. Gathering his tank top in a fist, I wrenched it up to bite a nipple on my way to his belly.

"What if we're caught?" Quinn asked with a gasp. He pulled off his tank top while I unbuttoned his shorts from my knees.

"I don't know." I pulled his trunks down and ran my tongue up the length of his erection, salty with the sweat of the day's walk. "What if we're caught?"

His fingers ran through my hair, gripping and tugging me forward. I hungrily took him, pushing his head against my tonsils, sucking and drawing my tongue under his length as I withdrew before sliding him back in.

He moaned and took a slow breath in. After so long together, I knew exactly how to work him.

"You think that cot could support two?" he whispered between deep breaths.

"I'd rather fuck you up in the lamp room," I said, except it came out as a slurred mumbled around his cock.

"Someone will definitely see us up there," he said, but I could see he was still considering it.

Suddenly, loud voices were immediately outside the door directly next to us. I bolted to my feet, yanking Quinn's trunks and shorts with me. There had to be a place to hide, but the room was nearly barren except—the wardrobe.

Quinn was already dragging me toward it. We yanked it closed with a clink just as the lighthouse door opened.

My eyes adjusted quickly in the musty space. We barely had room to shift an arm, but slats across the front gave a clear and wide view of the room. We watched the young gay boy who gave us the pamphlet enter, waving a hand to finish up a conversation and closing the door behind him. Not boy, he was clearly in his early twenties, but when you're pushing forty, those around twenty look like infants.

He grumbled something, dropping the stack of pamphlets on the table with the checkerboard and cards, and flopped into one of the chairs with a loud creak. He seemed to consider something for a moment, then got up and crossed to the door, dropping a beam over it, locking us in. Quinn tensed beside me, and I fully shared in the anxiety. There would be no way to slip away quietly. We were trapped in the wardrobe unless we wanted to make ourselves known. He returned to the chair but stopped before it, yanking off his belt and letting his linen pants drop to the floor. His legs were spread wide when he sat down with another creak. Quinn squeezed my wrist as the pamphlet kid tugged at his limp cock that grew with every stroke.

Quinn flashed me wide eyes and nodded toward the stranger as if to say, "We can't watch this, right?"

I shrugged and shook my head, "What can we do?" If he jerked off and left, it would just be a fun story for Quinn and me later. Hell, maybe even some roleplaying later with one of us hiding in the closet. But if he finished and came toward us, what then? That gets exponentially more difficult to explain.

The kid spit into his palm and kept working.

I was ready to make us known when he froze, hand by his mouth, eyes ready to pop from his skull as they focused on something on the floor.

Fuck. Quinn's tank top!

Martin's eyes darted across the room and quickly settled on the wardrobe. He jumped to his feet, turning and yanking his pants up.

Quinn forced a cough and pushed the wardrobe door open.

Martin looked mortified.

"Hey bro, this is awkward," Quinn said, forcing a chuckle.

"Did you..." Martin stepped around the chair, holding onto its back with both hands.

"We saw what you were doing," said Quinn.

"But we won't tell anyone," I added. "Truth is, we came in here to do the same."

"Well, for starters." Quinn winked at me.

"Starters?" Martin's shoulders relaxed.

I jerked a thumb at my husband. "Quinn was wondering if the cot could hold both our weight."

Martin looked to consider the cot for a breath, then let his gaze slip over us holding hands.

Quinn noticed the attention, too. "Benj likes to fuck me in odd places."

"An old lighthouse isn't that odd. The abandoned cemetery yesterday, maybe so." I raised his hand to kiss the back of it.

Quinn turned his attention back to Martin. "It's good you came in when you did. Another ten minutes and you would have walked into Benj's balls slapping my ass."

Too far, Quinn, but I had to roll with it. "Oh, honey, in ten minutes, we'd be done and walking through the market. How about you, Martin? What's your story?"

Martin stepped beside the chair, keeping one hand on its back. "I had to get away from that crowd. This town's just miserable."

"And you wanted a bit of... release," Quinn said.

Martin shrugged and nodded. "My manager wants to fire me for being gay. If he knew I was masturbating on the clock—"

"You're safe." I stepped to him and put a hand on his shoulder. "We interrupted each other, though. Should we shake hands and part ways?"

Quinn moved closer. "Or do we pretend the other party isn't there and continue what we were doing? Now the door's locked, no one else should be joining us."

The look of wide-eyed shock on Martin's face fueled a little giddy piece within me. I could see the engines revving, trying to decide what to do next.

"Although..." Quinn put a hand on Martin's other shoulder. "Weren't you just telling me the other day, Benj, that you'd never sucked a ginger's dick?"

"I'd never sucked a circumcised ginger's dick," I corrected him. We had never discussed anything of the like.

Quinn snapped his fingers. "That's right, sorry. It's up to you, Martin. Benj and I fuck over on the cot, the three of us see what's going on, or do nothing and leave."

"It's his lighthouse," I said. "We're not supposed to be in here. He could kick us out and jerk off alone as he planned. Do you want to kick us out, Martin?"

"Stay." Martin's voice was barely a raspy wheeze. He cleared his throat. "I want to watch."

Quinn stepped around behind me, slipping his hands under my tank top and pulling it up to expose my nipples. "Just watch? Benj could teach master-level classes in dick-sucking."

A bit of an oversell, but I'd never refuse a complaint.

"You..." Martin looked between us as one hand moved to his pants buckle. "You're okay with that?" His question was directed at Quinn.

"With my husband blowing another man? Few things are hotter."

Martin's fingers traced the steel button before pushing it through the hole and shaking his linen pants to the floor. His erection bulged under his boxers, barely staying behind the buttoned fly.

I slid my fingers down the elastic at his hips, curling my palm around the band as I stepped in front of him, tugging down the boxers while going to my knees.

"You can stop this at any moment," Quinn said. "Just say... Lighthouse."

His cock was only inches from my face, rooted in a thick patch of flaming red. I looked up at Martin, waiting for some confirmation of consent. He nodded, and I drove his cock down my throat until my nose was in his pubes. He gasped and stumbled back, but Quinn was there, wrapping one arm around Martin's waist and the other hand around his neck, nibbling at his ear and whispering who knows what into it.

Martin was thicker but shorter than Quinn. No matter. I opened my mouth a little wider, but he didn't choke me as badly. Precum oozed from him, and I lapped it from his head after every few dives. He moaned, and I soon felt his fingers move through my hair, gripping loosely as he shifted his hips with my timing.

"Save some for me," said Quinn.

Martin's hands loosened in my hair, and his slow thrusts stopped.

I sat back on my heels and wiped my mouth, looking up at Quinn as his shorts and trunks dropped to the floor. He stepped out of them and moved to lean over the table with the checkerboard and cards. Martin stepped behind him, one hand on his dick, ready to guide it into my husband's ass.

Martin hesitated.

I stood and slipped in behind him, dropping my shorts and trunks, pressing my hard cock against Martin's firm ass.

"Do it," I whispered into his ear. I slid a hand down his chest, to his wrist holding his dick, then pushed my hips into him, moving him closer to Quinn.

Martin swallowed hard and advanced, pressing his dick to Quinn's anus, wiping his precum around it. I pushed again, and Martin transferred that forward, pressing until I heard the familiar gasp from my husband. Martin tried to pull back, to give Quinn a moment to acclimate, but I kept the pressure with my cock against his crack. He pushed deeper. Quinn released a slow, loud exhale, and I knew Martin was fully inside him.

"Fuck, you're thick," he panted, glancing over his shoulder with a wink. "Give me what you got, big boy."

Martin pulled back, slow and easy, and pushed forward with just as much care. I couldn't see his face, but sweat broke out across his back and arms. The next was harder, then faster. A dozen strokes in, Quinn was gripping the far edge of the table, forehead bumping the rough wood top of it.

Martin paused. Reaching between us, he grabbed my cock and shifted it to slide between his legs, against his anus, and tap the back of his balls. Martin reignited his rhythm, slamming the full length of his girth into Quinn. The feeling was amazing, my cock sliding against him, slick with my precum.

He paused again and grabbed my dick, directing it to his hole.

"You want me to fuck you?" I asked, pushing my hips into him, feeling the air escape his lungs as I breached his ass. I held there, my lips at his neck, listening to his sharp breaths. His next words would either be "lighthouse" or a moan to continue.

He moaned, and I continued.

Pushing slowly, I only gave him a few inches, but that would be enough. Holding myself steady, I pressed, and Martin transferred that motion into Quinn. We found a careful rhythm of me fucking Quinn through Martin, letting this shy young man experience being a top and bottom simultaneously.

"Does that feel good?" I whispered across his ear.

He nodded slowly, turning back, biting his lower lip, eyes squeezed tight.

"Are you going to cum?"

He nodded, mouth dropping open with gasping breaths.

I pushed harder, faster, letting my cock slide just a little in him. Quinn held onto the table as it slid forward an inch with each thrust.

"Fuck!" Martin pressed forward and held. His orgasm rocked through to his knees, and I felt it tightening around my cock still inside him. I pulled out, and Martin collapsed forward onto Quinn's back. A few gasping breaths later, he stood and nearly fell over, if not for him grabbing the chair's back again.

Quinn rolled over, trusting his weight fully to the table.

"What about you two?" Martin gasped.

Quinn squeezed the ginger's dick. "How about Benj fuck me while you finish me off?"

I didn't wait for Martin's response but stepped up between Quinn's spread legs. One hand shot behind his neck to pull him forward for a kiss while the other held my dick. I pushed deep into him, his ass slick with the ginger's cum and stretched by his thick cock.

Martin scrambled between, working a hand around Quinn's dick, trying to get the angle to suck it, but not trusting the table with more weight.

The ginger worked between us, but Quinn and I only had eyes for the other. I skipped to the long, fast rhythm that I knew was grinding against Quinn's prostate, both from experience and how his lips parted to gasp his breaths.

He nodded once.

I was there, too. Trying my best not to break stride, I pumped into him as he shot his load at a surprised Martin, hitting almost to his collarbone. Still in him, I leaned to kiss Quinn, then slid free while our foreheads were pressed together.

Quinn leaned back, turning to Martin and gesturing at his chest and belly. "Do you have a rag or something?"

Martin's eyes went wide. "Yes, give me a second." He dashed to the wardrobe.

"I feel like we should help his lighthouse," Quinn whispered, lying back across the table.

"He certainly seems passionate about it."

"And we said if we won the lottery, we'd help fund people's passions."

"We did say that."

Quinn licked his lips. "Did I feel that right? You were inside him, inside me?"

"Pretty hot, right?"

"Goddamn, I wish we'd set up a tripod."

Martin returned with a few old straps of cloth that we used to clean up. Almost as a formality, Quinn told Martin where we were staying at Harborview Cove the next few nights, just in case he wanted to play around some more. Whether he did or not is another story, but the next time Quinn and I visited the little town five years later, the lighthouse was in perfect working condition, repairs paid by an unknown donor.

# Coach Nick

"3-6-5-4! 3-6-5-4! I WANT to see you explode! Don't hold anything back!"

I had nothing left to give as I feebly punched the heavy bag. Sweat dripped from my nose and chin with every punch. It made my pants cling to my shins and my shirt to my chest. Meanwhile, Coach Nick did the class at double anyone else's intensity, all while shouting encouragements into his headset. I turned up my power when I saw him approaching, stopping at the bag closest to mine. He beat the living shit out of it.

"Come on, Zack! You got more than that! Let me see it!"

Oh, I'd love to, Coach Nick. I'd love nothing more than exactly that.

I tried to match his ferocity, wailing on the bag, blowing out a grunt of air with every impact. With every punch, my back and shoulders burned with the exertion, sweat spattering the mats at my feet.

"Get your hips into it. Drive with the feet." He demonstrated, then slipped behind me after I tried to mimic him, pushing a glove into my right flank as I punched. I needed to do more incorrectly more often.

"Good! Yeah! Get it, Zack!" Coach Nick offered a glove, and I punched it before he moved on, weaving through the hanging bags and pausing to encourage the others in the class. My pace slowed as I watched him, shorter than me by almost a full head, but those shoulders, those arms, how his shirt clung to his back and across his pecs. He could break me in half, and I'd welcome it.

The class ended with a grueling core workout: planks, leg lifts, and more planks. Couch Nick announced mountain climbers, and I choked back a groan. Then, he was at my side, down in a high plank.

"Get those knees high, Zack. Pump it." He demonstrated a few, then jumped to his feet. I felt his hands on my hips, pushing them toward the mat. "Butt low." He kept his palms pressing into my hips as I did a few more reps. The final bell sounded, announcing the class's end. Coach Nick offered a hand down to me, and I took it. Gripping my palm around his thumb, he nearly lifted me from the floor with only his strength.

"Good work today, Zach." He offered his wrapped fist, and I tapped mine to it. His eyes lingered over me for half a breath before he moved off to thank the others in the class. Maybe it was just my imagination.

Taking my bag from the locker, I headed to the men's room. I'd shower at home, but if the fat flurries drifting down beyond the front windows were an indication, I didn't want to go out in clothes soaked through with sweat. I didn't know the names of anyone else in my weekly class, but the guy I thought of as "almost hot bald dude" was stepping away from the urinal, tucking back into his gray sweatpants as I entered the room. He gave me the standard half-nod on his way out.

The locker room followed some rules of threes. Three urinals, three stalls, three sinks, three shower stalls, three changing stalls, and a three-by-three grid of lockers. I stepped into one of the changing stalls, dropped my bag on the bench, and didn't bother to close the curtain as I wrestled the wet, clinging shirt over my shoulders. Digging through my bag, hunting for my hand towel, I could feel the sweat across my back drying quickly in the locker room's cool air.

"Good workout, Zach. Your form is getting better every week."

I glanced over my shoulder, Coach Nick walking directly toward me. He veered at the last second, pushing down the front of his track pants as he stepped in front of a urinal. Only the elbow-high partition separated us.

"Thanks. I think the workouts might be getting easier." While true, I still felt ready to die by the end of each one. My recovery was getting faster, though. I was barely sore the next day after last week's class. Giving up on finding my towel, I pulled the clean shirt from my bag and turned to him.

His eyes ran over me quickly, and he smirked. "Glad to hear it. Have you thought about private lessons?"

"Private?" I stepped forward, fiddling with the shirt in both hands, holding it in front of my stomach. "I didn't think the club offered those."

"They don't. But I do." Coach Nick focused forward and down, shaking and tucking in. It was only then that it really clicked in me that he'd been talking while holding his dick.

He stepped from the urinal, facing me, and no force in the world could stop me from glancing down at the bulge in his track pants. I lowered my shirt to hide the growing one in mine.

"Private lessons," I stammered. "Yeah, that sounds great. Here?"

He chuckled and ran a hand across his close-cropped scalp. "No, couldn't do it here for insurance reasons. I have a little setup in my loft."

"Oh, great." His green eyes pierced into mine, and I tugged on my shirt as an excuse to break it.

"I have another class, but give me your phone. Text me, and we'll set up a time."

After digging through my bag again, I handed him my cell, unlocking it as I did. Coach Nick tapped in his contact info and passed it back just as quickly.

"Gotta run. Text me." He left with a wink.

Watching him leave, his tight ass poured into those tight track pants; I couldn't read him. The wink was flirty, but why would someone with arms and an ass like his want to flirt with me? I looked at my phone, at the newly added contact. "Coach Nick" followed by a winky face with its tongue sticking out.

I didn't even know you could put an emoji in someone's contact. Goodness, Coach Nick had a lot to teach me.

I stared at that winky face for three days, going through a dozen drafts before finally sending a simple,

> Hey, this is Zach.

The response chimed a few moments later.

> Hey bud! You down for a private?

> Yeah! Just give me the when and where!

Too many exclamation marks. Oh well, my excitement was legitimate.

> Tomorrow 6 am?

He included an address about twenty minutes away in the city. Six in the morning? Really? I set my regular alarm for seven and smacked it off for the next one at eight. I could do one early day, rather than spend a half hour texting back and forth about schedules.

> See you then!

There had been no discussion of compensation, but I checked my wallet and counted enough twenties to cover anything reasonable.

There was plenty of street parking at 5:30 in the morning, especially on a Sunday, and I spent the next fifteen minutes chugging my coffee and catching up on emails.

> I'm a little early. Okay, if I come up?

I sent it when the minutes just dragged. They continued to drag without a response. I rode the dark elevator to the twenty-fourth floor and knocked on the heavy steel door at the end of the hall a few minutes shy of the hour. Heavy music thumped beyond, so far out of place for the early hour.

I raised my hand to knock again, this time turning my fist to pound, but it yanked inward, upsetting my balance. Powerful hands caught me by the hips before I could fall, and Coach Nick spun me to face him. Just as quickly, he flashed a grin and cut off the Eminem deep cut with a tap of the remote in his hand.

"Punctual," Coach Nick said, waving me in and closing the door. He was barefoot, wearing blue shorts half the length of his thigh to show off his leg hair and an oversized shirt from a gym with the sleeves cut off and sides slit to almost the bottom hem, exposing the lean muscle along his ribs. He was also dripping with sweat.

"I was a bit early, waiting in my car."

"You should have come up." He waved me in. His loft was a studio apartment out of a movie. High ceilings, exposed brick on the exterior walls, and huge windows overlooking the city. To the left, the kitchen, TV, and couch. To the right, a bed with pristine sheets and the only other interior door that probably led to the bathroom. Straight ahead was his neatly arrayed exercise equipment and a few heavy bags.

"Nice place." I dropped my bag on a weight bench and laid a palm on a worn bag bearing the marks of more than one patch job. I turned to him just as he straddled the weight bench while sucking down on a bottle of water.

"I've had a close eye on you, Zack, and I've noticed how you watch me in class. Like recognizes like. I think we can help each other out."

I tore my gaze from the water bottle nestled against his crotch, to his eyes. "Oh?" Fuck, he was coming out to me. This might actually happen.

"I've been where you are, and boxing helped pull me out of it," he said.

I felt my brows crinkle with my confusion.

"I was an addict for almost five years," he clarified, waving a hand. He shrank back with whatever look was on my face. "I'm sorry, I shouldn't have assumed."

"I'm not an addict." I chuckled, hoping to break the tension. "At least not to drugs."

"This is embarrassing." He ran a hand across his head. "I thought you were trying to get my attention."

There was no point in beating around the bush. "That's not why. You must realize you're easy on the eyes, Coach Nick."

"I've been told that. Wait, are you gay?" He cracked a grin, easing the tension.

I nodded.

"No shit."

"I'm sorry for staring."

Coach Nick waved it off. "It's flattering. I should be thanking you." He slammed the rest of his water and stood. "To be honest, I hoped to help you with the other thing, but let's do the private lesson you came for."

And we did exactly that. Even knowing I was gay and attracted to him, he touched my hips and shoulders just as much to correct my form. If anything, he stood a little closer while doing it. An hour later, I was unwinding my hand wraps and Coach Nick was asking me to come back at the same time next week.

"Let yourself in, even if you're early," he said.

I attended his normal class, and a week later brought us to another Sunday at 6 am, made extra terrible by daylight savings springing ahead an hour.

Walking from the elevator to his steel door in the pre-dawn hours, I heard no loud thumps of music from his loft. Maybe Coach Nick was being extra considerate since it was all an hour earlier than usual.

As he told me to, I entered without knocking, scanned the apartment, and saw him starfished on the bed with the sheets pushed down to his hips. I thought to step out and knock, but another part of me wanted to approach and watch Adonis sleep. The second thought was quickly swelling, tenting my shorts.

That won.

I'd shake his shoulder to wake him.

Before I did, I drank in the sight of Coach Nick. One hand was over his head on the pillow, showing a bulging bicep and a dark patch of pit hair. His own arm lay outstretched with his fingers curling to the ceiling. His pecs swelled and fell with his slow breath. A fine trail of short hair led from his chest, across a flat stomach, to somewhere under the cream-colored sheets. Those sheets were, unfortunately, too stiff to tell any detail other than a slight bulge between his legs.

I reached to touch his shoulder, started diverting to put a hand on his chest, but pulled back. Why should I wake him at all? He'd clearly forgotten about daylight savings, and I'd rob him of the sleep I didn't get. I'd text him, and we'd reschedule.

> Sorry! I forgot about dst! Can we reschedule?

Send.

I only made it a few steps from the bed when his phone dinged. Coach Nick inhaled deeply, eyes fluttering open. He yelped and rolled away from me, falling off the far side of the bed.

I ran around to help him, but he jumped to his feet in front of me.

Fully nude.

My eyes took in the deep cuts along his hips down to his completely shaved groin. His dick either looked engorged from the start of a morning rager, or he was big at rest.

"Zack!" Rather than attempt to cover himself, he fumbled for his phone on the nightstand. It was still a few minutes shy of 6, or 5 before the time change. "Dude! I'm so sorry!"

"No, it's my fault. I let myself in." I tried not, and failed, to stare at his growing erection and how his balls tucked up as he pointed directly at me.

"Give me two minutes. Put your wraps on, and I'll be right there." He stepped toward me, squeezed my elbows, and then walked past toward the kitchen. After a half dozen steps, he slowed and stopped, head hanging as he chuckled. "I'm naked."

I stared at his ass sculpted by a hundred daily squats. "I might have noticed."

He turned on a heel, clasping his hands to cover his crotch. "Well, this is highly unprofessional."

"I won't tell anyone." I folded my hands like he did to hide my erection.

"I appreciate that." He laughed nervously and moved to a pile of clothes beside the bed, careful to keep his hands in front of him until he bent to pull on a pair of loose shorts. "You know, I was actually relieved last week when you told me you're gay, not an addict. I was so set on what I'd say, that I was at a loss when I found out I was wrong."

I took a step back. "Why's that?"

"This'll sound stupid." He sat on the edge of his low bed and gestured for me to join him. "During my recovery, I've tried not to overlook gifts from the universe. I don't believe in actual cosmic gifts, but I try to seize opportunities and not take my time for granted."

"That sounds nice." I held a sham pillow in my lap in an attempt to look casual. I'd only seen Coach Nick at full intensity with his hands wrapped. Now I saw a gentle, calm side to him, and all I could think about was slipping a hand behind his neck and pulling him down on his bed as we kissed.

"If you needed a sponsor, Zack, I would have done it in a heartbeat. Few things would mean as much to me as pulling another from the darkness I was once in."

"But then..."

"Then you told me you're gay. It got me thinking, and I've spent the last week wondering if

I'm ready to take another step through recovery."

He didn't continue right away, so I asked, "What step is that?"

Coach Nick licked his lips and looked at me through his lashes. "I've been celibate for two years."

"Oh!" I drummed my fingers on the pillow. "Is this because I said you're hot? I figured you get that all the time. I'm trying my best not to let it affect us. Trying. Maybe failing."

He shrugged. "I should have said you're nice to look at, too."

"What? But you're..." I stammered. "Are you gay?"

He waggled his hand back and forth. "I appreciate the beauty of the male form and have some experience between the sheets. Or behind the dumpster at Long John Silver's." He grinned, but I was too hung up on his words to appreciate the humor.

I asked, "If you're ready to take a step forward, what's that next step?"

Coach Nick reached to trace a fingertip on my knee. "I'll make it up to you, but would you want to skip the lesson and go back to bed? Not for sex, just... be close."

I nodded, not trusting my words.

He was back under the sheets in a flash to watch me fumble my shirt over my head with clumsy fingers. Coach Nick lifted the sheets, and I slipped in beside him.

"Forty-five minutes," he said, rolling to put his phone on the nightstand. Rather than returning to his back, he scooted closer to me. I flipped to my side, pushing my right arm under his neck and letting the other fall across his ribs. Coach Nick scooted back again, pressing his back to my chest, heedless of my erection pressing firmly between his ass cheeks, which only encouraged me to actively push my hips against him. He took my hand across his side, laced his fingers through mine, and moved it low across his belly to brush the waistband of his shorts. I pulled my arm under him to hold him in a hug with my nose buried at the base of his neck. When I released and let my arm drop to the mattress, he placed his other on top of it.

Goddamn this escalated quickly. I nervously worshipped this man for weeks; now, there were few ways for us to be physically closer. I didn't think there was any way I'd fall asleep as I felt Coach Nick's breath slow against my chest, but the alarm woke us both with the sun starting to peek over the city skyline outside the windows. He smacked it off and flopped back into me. A breath later, he was wiggling in place, rolling to face me without creating much distance between us.

"That was nice," he said, putting a warm hand across my side. He stroked a toe along the side of my foot.

This close, I noticed the flecks of silver at the edge of his irises catching in the early light.

I shot forward, pressing my lips to his. If he was shocked, it didn't last long. His hand at my side tightened, pulling us close so I could feel how hard he was through the loose shorts. His tongue slid over my lips and I parted them to let him in.

With a smooth motion, Coach Nick threw a knee over me, mounting me with our fronts in unbroken contact. His fingers laced through mine and pulled my hands over my head as we kissed with lips and tongues, almost savage with our efforts.

He shifted from my lips to my cheek and then my neck, eliciting a gasp from my throat and a chill down my spine. He moved along my collarbone, biting at my nipple, and dragged his tongue along my ribs. His nose tickled a path down, down, down until he hovered over my member. He wasted no time, lightly biting, gauging my size through my shorts. It had to be soaked through with precum. Warm hands slid from my knees, up my thighs, into my shorts, and under my trunks, tracing a gentle finger down either side of my cock on their way back out.

Coach Nick kissed and licked his way back up to me.

"I want you, Zack," he breathed into my ear.

I rolled us so I was on top. Tracing the same path he did on me, I tried to have his patience as I moved, but my fingers were in the waistband of his shorts before I knew it. He bridged his hips, and I yanked them down.

I thought he was beautiful before, in the dim pre-dawn light, but being inches from his manhood was nearly enough to make me cum. I ran my tongue across his smooth balls, up his shaft, and used a hand to angle him into my mouth. Coach Nick gasped and moaned my name when I took him. Working his shaft with one hand, cupping his balls with the other, and focusing my mouth and tongue on his head. His breath quickened, and he moaned my name again, this time more as a whimper. His fingers raked through my hair. Keeping one hand around his sack, I drove his cock to my tonsils, savoring his sweet precum.

My hand slipped between his legs, preparing to seek his asshole, but he grunted, "Fuck!" and shot his hot load against the back of my throat. I returned all focus to his cock, savoring the shutters and quakes along with enough seed that I had to swallow twice. When he seemed done, I looked up at him with his arms spread, chest heaving and glistening with sweat.

His gaze was on the ceiling, but he quickly craned his neck to look down at me with a broad grin. He crooked a finger, beckoning, and I crawled up him. One hand slipped behind my neck, pulling me close to kiss. The other snuck between us to grip my cock.

"Your turn."

He'd been so gentle and vulnerable all morning that it was easy to forget Coach Nick's raw strength. He pushed me back, forcing me upright over him, then wrapped powerful hands around my knees to drag me until I straddled his chest. He licked his lips and focused an expectant gaze on my cock in front of him.

I worked myself in earnest, surprised I hadn't spilled already. When he opened his mouth and extended his tongue, eager for my offering, I was done in. My stream shot across his neck and cheek, across his left eye. A little hit the corner of his mouth, which he lapped up immediately. His hand snaked behind my neck again, pulling me helplessly forward at an awkward angle to kiss him, neither of us caring about the cum smearing between us.

After cleaning up, we finally got to that private lesson, though shirtless.

I continued attending his boxing classes, and if any other students noticed something between us, no one ever said a thing.

I let myself into his loft and his bed every Sunday, where we'd sleep a bit longer in each other arms before finding new ways to pleasure the other. On the third week, he gave me a condom and a hopeful look. I gave him the same the following week. There was no surface in his apartment that one of us hadn't pinned the other against.

I wouldn't have been able to guess how long this could go on, but the answer was seven weeks. After two months of our quiet trists, the pure lust faded, and I wanted more from the man. I found myself lying on the couch at night, thinking of him beside me. I wanted to go to the movies or dinner with him. To take a walk in the park.

I was balls deep in him when this hit me, as I worked a slow rhythm with our foreheads pressed together and slick with sweat. He arched his head back, letting a tiny moan escape, and I knew all that I had from this man, this Adonis, wasn't enough.

With my speech rehearsed, I entered his loft the following Sunday, ready to end things if this was all we'd be.

He was already dressed and sitting on the edge of his bed, preparing to tell me all the same.

We ended up laughing about it and then going to a matinee. I never understood why someone who looked like him would want to be with someone like me. I saw nothing special in me, but he claimed the same in him. I worshiped Coach Nick as a living god, and by how he couldn't keep his eyes or hands off me, I knew he felt the same for me.

# Also By Dirk

**Other works by Dirk Mourningwood**
La Luce's Legacy (2024)
Eros Unzipped (2024)
Eros Unchained (2024)

# About Dirk

Dirk Mourningwood is an emerging voice in the world of MM erotica, known for his bold storytelling and captivating characters. With a passion for exploring the depths of human desire and the complexities of male relationships, Dirk weaves tales that are both sensual and emotionally resonant. His writing invites readers into a world where passion knows no bounds and love transcends all barriers. When he's not crafting his next tantalizing story, Dirk enjoys immersing himself in period dramas, practicing kenjutsu, and playing disc golf with his lab Rodger.